W9-BBO-851

9/8/2005

WITHDRAWN
No longer the property of the
Boston Public Library.
Sale of this material benefits the Library

Ben Cooper, U.S. Marshal

**This Large Print Book carries the
Seal of Approval of N.A.V.H.**

Ben Cooper, U.S. Marshal

Phillip Underwood

Thorndike Press • Thorndike, Maine

Library of Congress Cataloging in Publication Data:

Underwood, Phillip.
  Ben Cooper, U.S. marshal / Phillip Underwood.
     p. cm.
  ISBN 1-56054-141-5 (alk. paper : lg. print)
  1. Large type books. I. Title. II. Title: Ben Cooper,
US marshal.
[PS3571.N438B4   1991]   91-2096
813'.54—dc20   CIP

All the characters and events portrayed in this work are
fictitious.

Thorndike Press Large Print edition published in 1991
by arrangement with Walker Publishing Company, Inc.

Cover design by Sean Pringle.

The tree indicium is a trademark of Thorndike Press.

This book is printed on acid-free, high opacity paper. ∞

For My Mother
Helen Judith Underwood

CHAPTER 1

For eight years Ben Cooper had been a federally appointed marshal of Mexican Hat, Utah. The weight of the badge upon his chest rested easy. He coped with the hazardous duties of his job by using his wits and powers of persuasion — if that failed, his huge fists or his gun. He used violence as a last resort, preferring to give his opponent every chance to surrender peaceably as Cooper pointed out to the miscreant the brevity of life itself. More than one would-be gunfighter had backed down after staring for an eternal moment into the twin black eyes of Cooper's shotgun.

His reputation had grown through the years to where most of the desperadoes roaming the Southwest gave Mexican Hat a wide berth. An occasional bout with comancheros and one attempted holdup of the Cattleman's First National Bank and Trust, in which three bandits and one deputy were left dead and Cooper himself gravely wounded, seemed to put a cap on the violence in the area for a while.

Cooper's routine, after he recovered from his wounds, settled into a pattern of placid, even-flowing days. His need for deputies dwindled until only one was kept on the payroll: Cecil Akins, himself a former sheriff, and a man with the tact and even temper needed to keep the rowdies in line without bloodshed. In short, a man after Cooper's own heart.

Throughout the tumultuous years, Cooper's closeness to Jane Porter had grown. She was a distinctively fine-figured woman, with a strong and graceful stride. Her hair was long, dark, and lustrous, and she fastened it up with her silver combs only when she was at work.

She owned and ran a restaurant patterned after some of the more exquisite restaurants in Santa Fe. But, wisely, she served good, homey meals, with local tastes in mind. It was a successful, thriving establishment — only Marshal Ben Cooper was assured of a place to sit at any given meal.

On the anniversary of his becoming marshal, Cooper was surprised by Jane's presenting him with a gift while he sat in the restaurant.

"Before we begin," Jane said sweetly, "let me assure you, Ben Cooper, I had serious doubts about this."

Cooper looked at the package doubtfully.

It was a long, wide box, festooned with bright ribbons and bows.

He looked from the package to her face, a skeptical smile on his lips. "If this isn't from you, who —"

"Oh, it's from me, all right. I just wasn't sure about the thing. If you must know, it was suggested to me by Cecil. He somehow thought it would be appropriate — something you could use." Her cheeks reddened slightly and she went on. "Actually, we all felt you should have something to commemorate the day — the beginning of your ninth year as marshal." She smiled nervously, and clasped and unclasped her hands beneath the drape of tablecloth.

"Do I open it now?" he asked with a wary smile.

Cooper, Jane, Deputy Akins, and several others sat near the center of the restaurant. Upon the table before them lay the remains of a small chocolate cake — baked and decorated by Jane — and a nearly empty wine bottle. Well-wishers hung about the table, their smiles growing tired.

"Of course. Open it," she ordered. "It won't do anybody any good in the box."

He slipped the ribbons aside and opened the box. Inside, glistening in its oiled newness, lay a gunbelt of black, tooled leather. Gleaming silver conchos were in the spaces between the loops of the cartridge belt. One large, dollar-sized concho was riveted to the holster itself.

"Ooee, Ben," exclaimed Tank McFarland from the next table. "You'll look plumb fit to dance in that rig. That's purty." And a hearty guffaw rolled forth.

Confusion appeared in Jane's eyes. She looked uncertainly from Cooper's face to the gunbelt.

"Say, this is great," said Cooper quickly, but the damage was done. Spots of fiery red shown against the smooth whiteness of Jane's cheeks. She opened her mouth to speak, but then closed it again sharply. An embarrassed silence hung over the room like a shroud.

Cooper reached across the table, seized her delicate hand and squeezed her fingers. "Jane, don't listen to that fool Tank. It's a wonderful gift, and I'll cherish it always." He was grinning broadly as he spoke.

"Ben, you've been wearing that old gunbelt ever since you been big enough to strap one on," said Cecil Akins. "Why, look at the old thing. The stitchin' wore out. The cartridge loops is pullin' out of the leather. Hell, Ben, you're damn near ready to lose your gun altogether."

"Listen, you two," said Cooper, resolutely

unbuckling his old gunbelt and slapping it on the table. "It was a fine idea, and I really do appreciate it." He slipped his six-gun into the new, stiff leather, stood up and buckled on the new gunbelt.

Cooper looked at Tank McFarland with a grin loaded with evil intent. "And if I hear one more crack out of you, I'm going to have Janey cut your rations in half."

A shocked look appeared on Tank's face, and he spread both hands protectively across his ample stomach.

"That's exactly right," exclaimed Jane. "If you ever make fun of my tastes again, Tank —"

"No, ma'am," said Tank meekly.

Cooper reached across the table, clasped Jane's hand, and led her through the loud talk and joking to the door. "Come on. Let's get some air," he said. She followed him gratefully.

Once outside and alone except for casual traffic on the dusty street, Cooper stopped and turned to her. He held her at arm's length, looked down into that flawless face which reflected back to him an open and honest love, and his mind spun and his heart took a sickening lurch as he felt the same old doubts and discontent wash over him.

It would be so much easier, he counted, if

he could simply tell her, and himself, that he did not love her; or maybe say to her that he just didn't feel that they would be right for each other — not for a lifetime together, anyway. But that, he realized with an abrupt jolt of self-disgust, would be the biggest sham of all. If it was not love he felt for Jane Porter, it was the closest thing likely to come along in the life of Ben Cooper. He could not imagine anyone easier to get along with on a day-to-day basis than Jane. But somehow that wasn't enough for Cooper. Even worse, he was afraid Jane knew it wasn't enough, although Cooper couldn't even admit it to himself.

She stood there a moment, a quizzical half-smile on her lips, confusion in her eyes. And then, as he watched, her eyes seemed to open wider, the smile faded, and a sadness like cold white wax set upon her features.

She took an imperceptible step backward, and his arms fell from her shoulders to his sides. He knew then that the look on her face was a reflection of his own.

"I'd better get back to work, Ben," she said softly. Reaching up to him she kissed him softly on the lips, then turned and retreated into the restaurant, leaving him standing alone.

CHAPTER 2

It was midmorning, the first day of October, and the Utah sun was blistering away, cracking and peeling the green scum at the edge of the stagnant pond. A ewe goat, ponderous teats dragging, drank at the water's edge.

The cabin was built upon stilts three feet from the ground. A small black dog was curled in the shade beneath the plank steps. Above the steps was a sign proclaiming the sale of groceries, whiskey, ammunition, and dry goods.

Inside, the atmosphere was dank and gloomy as a cave, the light struggling feebly through the two small fly-specked windows in front. Against a side wall filled with canned goods, a large fat man leaned on his elbows against a plank bar, reading a newspaper several weeks old. A few wisps of gray hair wandered at will on the otherwise bald head. As he read he scratched at a rash above one ear. He was shirtless, his pants supported by soiled red suspenders pressing deeply into the flesh of his bare shoulders. He smelled bad.

In a corner a Ute woman lay sleeping on a blanket spread on the floor. She lay on her back with her mouth open, snoring softly.

The sharp yapping of the dog broke into the fat man's concentration, and he looked up from the newspaper with rheumy, reddened eyes.

Four men on horseback were skirting the pond when he reached the window at the end of the bar. A jab of fear shot through him; he didn't like the looks of these men. They rode weary horses, four abreast, and their faces bore the stamp of desperation and cruelty.

They tied their horses at the hitchrack, and one, the oldest appearing, spotted the fat man's face in the window. The cold black eyes pierced to the fat man's heart.

The dog barked furiously at the legs of one of the men, a bearded scowling giant in dust-covered overalls and a soiled sheepskin vest. The man pulled a coiled blacksnake whip from his saddle and, fast as lightning, laid its length across the dog's back. One yelp and the dog disappeared like a ghost into the shadows beneath the house.

"Woman!" the fat man whispered, tearing his gaze from the window.

The Indian woman snored on, and the fat

man spun with surprising agility and hurried to her sleeping form.

"Woman! Get up!" he ordered, glancing quickly over his shoulder at the men who were just mounting the porch steps. The woman's eyes fluttered, closed again. She rolled comfortably over with her back to the fat man. In a panic the man delivered a kick to her generous buttocks.

"Drunken swine! On yer feet!"

The woman, now fully awake, crawled swiftly away on hands and knees and cowered in the corner, glaring at the fat man with fear and hatred in her black eyes.

The thump of heavy boots on the plank floor brought the man's head around. A sickish smile spread across his fleshy lips.

"You be Sinclair?" one of the men called out as they walked to the bar. The one who spoke laid the blacksnake on the bar, his stony gaze never leaving the fat man's face.

"That'd be me," the fat man replied genially. "This here's my woman. Woman, get these men dished up some of them beans." He moved quickly behind the bar.

"First drink's on the house, boys. Homemade and the best you'll find this side of the mountains." He placed tin cups on the bar and poured a generous dollop in each from a crock jug. "Drink 'em down there, boys.

Good fer what ails ya."

The eyes of the four bore steadily into the fat man, impaling him like a bug on a pin. Sinclair sweated and writhed.

"Yes, sir, by God! Being it's my birthday next week, I might jus' buy you fellows another round." He grinned hopefully. He knew their kind meant bad trouble.

"We be lookin' fer one by the name of Hinkle." It was the old man who spoke. His voice was deceptively soft and throaty, and it reminded the quaking Sinclair of the wind in the tops of the pines. He was a gaunt old man with eyes set deep in hollow sockets. He wore a long dark brown coat in spite of the wilting heat, and he appeared to be not the least uncomfortable for it. A broad-brimmed hat shielded his face.

"We need this Hinkle," the old man continued. "We was told he buys his necessaries from you."

Sinclair swallowed hard. He looked at the Indian woman, who had remained huddled in the corner.

"Hinkle. Hinkle." Sinclair gazed at the far wall, avoiding the four pairs of cold eyes. "I . . . we don't ask a man his name too often," he offered lamely. "'Course, if'n he offers it, that's somethin' else." His mind was at work with an alacrity surpassing the simple light

16

in his eyes. He was figuring the risks of somehow working these men for a price, making them pay for the information they sought.

"He's an old man," said the one with the whip. "Old man 'bout sixty-five. Small built. Might have a girl child with him."

"Rings a bell. Rings a bell. Say, you boys drink up there. You haven't touched yer drinks."

"We didn't come to drink," said the old man. His voice seemed even more gentle than before. Something dangerous here, thought Sinclair. A rattlesnake gliding over a rock. "We be needin' this Hinkle. We want to know where he's holed up. You can tell us now, the easy way, or you can tell us later."

The fat man's eyes widened. Sweat trickled from his armpits and ran down his fat sides.

"Hold on, boys," he laughed heartlessly. "I ain't holdin' out on ya. Honest to God. I'm tryin' to recall the fella — honest I am!"

Thoroughly terrified, Sinclair still held out the hope of an opportunity for some kind of gain. All his life he had thrived on borderline situations where the difference between profit and sudden death could be measured in inches. And he prided himself on his judgment of people. In this case, he felt he might be able to talk a deal with these men if he could get them to loosen up some.

"I got a twinge of somethin' in my memory. But it's been some time back. Just give me a little time here."

One of the men stood far shorter than the others. He was slight of build, with a fair lightly-bearded face but the same cruel eyes as the others. He leaned close and spoke into the older man's ear.

"Don't talk nonsense, boy," replied the older man. "We ain't got time fer fun like that."

The fat man's features brightened. "What's that? The boy spotted my woman, huh?" He tossed a glance at the woman in the corner. She had drawn the blanket up about her. She understood English.

"Go ahead, sonny," offered Sinclair, jerking a thumb at the woman. "Go ahead an' take her. You boys are welcome to anything I got, I want you to know." He smiled broadly. "At the same time, I ask ya to remember, I'm a binness man. Fair and reasonable — but still I'm in binness to make a livin'."

Something told Sinclair he had overplayed his hand. A great knot of fear seized his throat.

"We ain't interested in yer woman or yer goddamn business. We're interested in Hinkle." The old man motioned to the one with the whip.

A loop of leather snaked out and encircled

18

Sinclair's neck. He was pulled forward over the bar, and the fat man found his air flow cut off as the leather twisted and tightened. His eyes bulged from their sockets as his flesh took on a purplish suffusion.

After what seemed an eternity, the old man lifted his hand, and the leather noose was slackened to where Sinclair could pull air into his starved lungs.

While the bearded one with the whip held him draped across the bar, the old one drew a knife from his belt and laid the point on Sinclair's naked chest.

"Now," the old man whispered, "do ye got a clear understandin' of how bad we want to find Hinkle? Ye say ye be a *binnessman*. Here's a *binness* proposition fer ye. Tell us where Hinkle abides an' we kill ye quick."

The knife blade moved slowly across Sinclair's flesh, tracing a dripping red line from nipple to nipple. The fat man would have screamed had not the whip cinched tight again, cutting off his air.

CHAPTER 3

Along this stretch of eastern Utah, if the air was right, a man could see a hundred miles. Dust clouds and devils danced among the clumps of sage. Pools of blue water shimmered on the horizon, cool phantoms in the blistering heat. To the west were stacked the painted buttes, carved by ancient water and wind to expose layer upon layer of colored strata: browns, pinks, blush. To the east began the gradual incline of the foothills, swelling bosomlike to the peaks of the San Juans, lost for the moment in the distant haze.

Christie Hinkle spotted the horsemen when they were still many miles off. She watched the dancing shadows while the foal nibbled at her fingers. The paint mare, standing a few feet away, raised her head and nickered softly, catching the scent of the approaching horses.

At fifteen, Christie was already wise to the ways of the desert. The unknown was the enemy, dangerous always, until proven otherwise.

She caught up the lead rope and led the mare back to the small pole corral while the foal frolicked and bobbed behind. When the horses were within and the gate latched securely, she turned and plodded back to the adobe house. She found a comfortable spot in the shade next to the building and settled down to watch the approaching riders.

She was a pretty girl, with curly sandy-blond hair braided in pigtails on either side of her handsomely shaped head. Freckles were sprayed across her small upturned nose. Blond lashes veiled eyes blue and wise.

She wore old jeans with holes in either knee and frayed cuffs, a long-sleeved shirt made by the Navajos from bright vermilion cloth. Her feet were bare and covered with healed cuts and callouses.

She watched the distant riders floating ghostlike on the rising heat waves. Except for their slight rise and fall over the softly undulating ground, they appeared almost to be standing still.

Christie shaded her eyes with a palm and watched for several minutes. The shadows of the adobe grew long.

Abruptly the riders dropped from sight into an arroyo, and she watched intently for them to reappear. When they did not, she rose swiftly to her feet.

21

"Hap," she called softly.

A soft step from inside the house, and a white-whiskered face appeared in the open doorway.

"Riders," she said without looking up.

The man's eyes were washed-out blue, set into a mask of wrinkled leather. A mop of white hair hung like a lion's mane to his shoulders. He was not tall, scarcely taller than the girl, but his shoulders and chest were bunched with heavy muscle.

He rubbed his chin thoughtfully. "Cain't spot 'em, little gal."

"They dropped into the wash and didn't come out."

Together they watched and waited.

Finally the man sighed heavily. "We got troubles."

He looked at the sky. The sun was eclipsed by a butte, casting the area surrounding the house into an early dusk.

"We best remain right here, I guess," he said. "Being as it's so close to dark. Go take care of the stock, Christie. Get us in some extra water and then scoot yourself into the house as fast as ya can."

While the girl jumped to obey, the old man turned back into the house. He crossed the clean-swept plank floor to a gun rack mounted on the wall, took down a Winchester, and began thumbing cartridges into the breech.

He took down a belt containing a six-gun and a long-bladed sheath knife, and was buckling it about his slim waist when the girl returned for the water buckets.

"Don't tarry now," he cautioned, and then added a wink at the girl's sober face. "Not to worry, little gal. They ain't caught us nappin', now did they?"

The girl hurried toward the door.

"Christie," the old man called after her, "you done real good — spottin' 'em early like that."

The girl didn't answer but hurried on, ears flushed with pride.

While he waited for her to return, the old man went about the small, neat room, closing and barring the shutters, sorting out extra ammunition.

When all was in readiness, he paused. He thought for a moment and then dropped to all fours and reached under his bunk for a long narrow wooden box. From the box he extracted several sticks of dynamite, caps, and short fuses. This material was laid out on the floor below a window, out of the line of fire.

He quickly reviewed his preparations. Everything had been done. All that remained was the waiting.

He stood quickly looking to the open door, rifle in hand.

"Christie! Gal, you shake a leg. It's damn near dark right now . . ."

Twenty feet away in the gathering gloom stood the girl. A man stood behind her, pinioning her arms. A knife blade lay across her throat beneath her upturned chin.

A voice, a gravelly whisper said, "I guess maybe ye forgot that gully come out just below the animal shelter." The girl struggled. "Easy, missy. I don't be wantin' to slit that pretty throat."

The old man raised the rifle slowly.

"Go ahead," came the whispered challenge. "If ye think ye be faster'n this knife."

The old man hesitated.

"Drop it."

He hesitated a moment, and then laid the rifle in the dust at his feet.

"Now the gunbelt."

The old man complied.

"Ye be Hinkle?" asked the voice.

The old man nodded.

The knife was removed from the girl's throat and raised high in the air. A signal.

"Come on in, boys. They be ours now."

CHAPTER 4

Akins was middle-aged, portly, and yearning for retirement. Until his late thirties he had made a few futile attempts at farming at various locations around the Southwest. But a couple of factors called for change. First was a nagging wife who could not bear the insecurity of irregular income. Second, and most important, Cecil hated the hard work and long hours that farming demanded.

Twenty years ago he had become a lawman on the misinformation that it was an easy life requiring little physical effort, demanding only that one put in an appearance now and then.

In his first month as a sheriff in Arizona Territory, he had caught two bullets in the chest. Nine months later a mob had beaten him senseless and lynched the prisoner he had nearly forfeited his life defending.

At that point — or somewhere during his recovery — Akins got down to business. Again on the streets, he walked his rounds with a sawed-off shotgun draped across his arm. In the next year he killed five men, jailed countless others, and presided at the hangings of three of the territory's most notorious killers. And *then* the job became easy.

He remained sheriff of the same small town for sixteen years. When his wife died, he quit his job and moved to Mexican Hat, where he became deputy under United States Marshal Ben Cooper.

For four years he had worked under Cooper, relieved at having another man call the shots for a change. In Mexican Hat his life had taken on the ease he had been searching for when he left farming. As his waistline had grown, so had his contentedness.

When trouble occasionally did arise, he accepted it philosophically, going about his duties competently and without complaint.

Murder was a little different. Especially the murder of the helpless.

He rode behind the wagon bearing the bodies of Sinclair and the Ute woman. Whoever had done this piece of work, he stewed, had done a thorough job of it — had really gotten into their work. The bodies had been mutilated, and from their appearance the victims had been alive for much of it.

Akins shuddered. He had not seen work like this since he was a boy in Texas and

26

had viewed bodies as they were brought into town after a Comanche massacre.

The little black dog riding in the wagon beside the dead man looked back at the deputy, wagged his matted tail, and whined.

"Poor little feller. Looks like you were the only lucky one out today."

The little dog wagged his tail once more, circled, and lay down in a nest between the canvas-draped bodies.

When they reached town, Akins directed the driver to stop the wagon before the marshal's office.

The door of the small brick building opened, and Marshal Ben Cooper emerged. He was a big man, over six feet, with long, muscular arms and a deep, bull-like chest. His hair and eyes were black, his skin tinted with a trace of Cherokee ancestry. He had a calm, almost weary, ruggedly handsome face.

Cooper crossed the plank sidewalk in two long strides. He lifted the canvas cover. "What we got?"

"That old gunrunner, Sinclair, and his woman. Looks like they was guests of honor at a cattle stampede."

The marshal nodded, jaws set. "Someone worked the woman over with a blacksnake."

"Uh huh. An' whoever used the knife on

ol' fat boy here was a real surgeon. What leads a man to do things like that to another human, Coop?"

Cooper shook his head. "Meanness, I guess. How did the place look?"

"Tore up. Stuff scattered hell to breakfast. Took guns and ammunition, I'd guess. There weren't no money to be found neither." Akins toyed with his long mustache, tugging at the ends. "Ya know what I think? I think robbery was a second thing. First off, they was after their hides. They wanted something else out of 'em."

The dog, wagging his tail uncertainly, eased over carefully in the wagon, close to where the marshal stood. Cooper reached out a hand and scratched the dog behind the ears.

"Dog was hangin' around the place when we drove up," said Akins. "Must've belonged to Sinclair."

Cooper flipped the canvas back over the bodies.

"Figured I might as well keep the little scavenger around, if ya don't mind. What d'ya think, Coop?"

Cooper looked up at the deputy. "Keep him out from underfoot." He rapped on the side of the wagon. "All right, Corky," he said to the driver. "Take 'em on over. Tell Moss to

28

send the bill to the county."

Akins dismounted and scooped the dog from the wagon's tailgate.

"You stick around with ol' Cecil for a while, pardner," he told the animal, setting it gently on the ground. "You can be the deputy's deputy."

Cooper smiled at the unlikely scene. "Remember one thing," he warned. "If he starts demanding wages, it's coming out of your salary."

Cooper rode out to the store and dismounted. He tied the steeldust to the hitchrack, lifted his canteen from the saddle, and drank while his eyes roamed over the plank structure and the surrounding ground. He noticed, as he rode in, the tracks of the four horses riding abreast. Now, standing by the hitchrack, he paid careful attention to the individual tracks of the four men, taking care not to confuse the boot prints with those Cecil Akins and Corky Handle had made when they picked up the bodies.

Akins had pointed out that one of the four had worn moccasins. That fact might make identification easier later on.

The tracks led first into the cabin, and then a reverse, overlapping set had eventually led the four horses to the pond for water.

Cooper mounted the cabin steps slowly,

eyes alert and probing into the shadowed interior.

He stepped quickly aside as he entered and waited in the shadows until his eyes grew accustomed to the gloom.

A tin can rolled on the plank floor, followed by the scurrying of tiny rodent feet. From somewhere above came the soft flutter of wings.

Cooper identified each sound automatically, allowing nothing to detract from his alertness.

The place was as Akins had described it — in shambles. The bodies had been found, lashed horizontally, head to head on the plank bar.

Cooper ran a hand over the bloodstained wood, picked up a piece of slashed rope. Another piece of rope lay at his feet. He stooped to pick it up and chanced to glance at the underside of the bar. One section bore deep scratch marks where frantic fingernails had clawed.

The marshal stood up and drew a deep breath. This type of thing was not new, but it had been a few years since he had run into it. Whoever had performed these killings carried a sickness and needed to be caught up quickly. They were infected with a blood lust worse than any wild animal.

He made his way through the building,

searching for anything that might help him identify the killers. Cast-off bottles of a good quality whiskey — not the kind Sinclair was noted for passing around — ground out cigarettes, chairs placed about in a lounging fashion. The four had remained for quite some time, apparently enjoying themselves, and yet nothing in the way of hard evidence had been left behind. They had been wary.

He returned to his horse, gathered the reins, and followed on foot the tracks leading to the pond. In the damp soil at water's edge were the cleanly defined prints of all four men, along with good, deep impressions of the horses' hooves.

The moccasin prints were small, those of either a small man or a woman. The other three wore large boots with flat heels and block toes. There were no distinguishing marks on the horses' prints.

Cooper mounted the steeldust and walked the horse over the tracks leading away from the pond. He followed the tracks due east for a half mile and then pulled to a stop.

"It's going to be a long one," he told the horse. "They're headed into the buttes."

The horse's ears twitched at the man's voice. The animal blew once and, seeming to comprehend his master's thoughts, turned of his own volition for town.

CHAPTER 5

When he entered the office, Cooper found Cecil Akins at the desk, hunched over a stack of wanted posters.

"Not a thing here that I can see," Akins intoned matter-of-factly. "Just a long shot. I was looking for four that usually run together. All we got is their goddamn footprints, unless you come up with somethin' else."

Cooper threw his saddlebags on the desk. "Do me a favor. Throw some grub and cartridges in the bags for me. Enough for three, four days."

He estimated he had three good hours of daylight — enough to get lined out on the trail. If it didn't rain, which didn't look likely at the moment, and if the wind didn't blow the tracks away — a more likely prospect — and if they weren't moving too fast, he shouldn't have a lot of trouble overtaking the killers.

He left the office and crossed the street, pausing to let a buggy pass, and touched the brim of his hat at the pretty smiling woman sitting beside the somber driver.

The small diner was nearly empty. The supper crowd had not yet begun to drift in.

He chose a table in the corner, dropped his hat on an extra chair, and sat down with his back to the wall.

Jane walked over slowly and took the chair opposite. "You're early." Her dark brows raised questioningly.

He smiled back uneasily. "How good a mood are you in?"

Her smile was indulgent. "Let's have it. Our dinner's off?"

"Yes. I've got to go find some people."

She sighed and glanced down at her hands, folded in her lap. "Well" — she shrugged — "it's not as though I don't get to see you every day. Every time you come over to eat."

They looked at each other tentatively.

"What is it this time?" she asked. "Those bodies Cecil brought in?"

Cooper nodded. "I'm after four men. Or maybe three men and a woman. They rode off toward the buttes."

"Let me bring you some supper before you leave," she said, and left without waiting for his reply. Within minutes she returned with a full plate of steaming food.

Jane watched the man as he shoveled in the

meat and potatoes. He was a big, healthy man and he ate accordingly. And she liked that. He was not handsome, but his features were formed with an effulgence of strength and character that made him look good and made him the subject of women's scrutiny. When they went places together, Jane Porter was proud to be seen with him. To her that was important.

He looked up suddenly, a forkful of carrots poised midway between plate and mouth.

"Something on your mind, lady?" he asked, chewing thoughtfully.

She smiled wistfully and shook her head. "Nope. Not a thing."

He stopped chewing and looked at her strangely.

"You be real careful," she said softly. "I don't think I could get along without you."

"I'll be careful," he said.

The steeldust waited, hitched to the rack in front of Cooper's office. His loaded saddlebags and bedroll were tied behind the saddle.

Cecil Akins was seated in a chair he had taken from the office and placed on the boardwalk by the door. Tilted back on two chair legs, he was comfortably contemplating the street traffic. Sinclair's little black dog lay curled next to the deputy's chair.

"Want me to round up a couple men an' come along?" he asked as the marshal checked and loaded his Winchester and then rammed it down into the saddle boot.

"Now just who did you have in mind? I can't think of a soul who could be gone for more than a day. And as for you, you're going to be watching the town."

"Let's see," Cecil said wryly, figuring on his fingers. "That leaves just you. An' in case you forgot, there's four of them."

Cooper grinned. "I ain't scared." He looked at his deputy closely. "Besides, I had it in mind to take your dog along — if it meets with your approval."

Akins looked up, his face betraying concern. He swallowed and grinned helplessly. "Why ... sure, Coop. Take 'im. Might help ya out." He slowly lowered the front legs of his chair.

"He'd save me some time, Cecil," Cooper explained.

"Sure. You betcha," the deputy answered quickly, looking down at the dog snoozing between his legs. "Bet he'll make a damn good tracker." He nudged the sleeping dog with a toe. "Been callin' 'im Fang. I thought it kind of funny 'cause he ain't got balls the size of respectable peas." He nudged the sleeping dog again. "Get yer lazy butt up, dog. Time ya started earnin' yer keep."

Already Cooper regretted asking for the dog. It was plain that Akins had formed an attachment for the animal.

Cooper sighed. "On second thought, I might end up carryin' him across the saddle. Keep 'im. If he makes any messes in the office, you damn well better have 'em cleaned up before I get back."

CHAPTER 6

He started from Sinclair's deserted store and followed the tracks of the four horsemen until night fell. He made his camp on the slopes of a dry wash where large boulders would shield a small campfire.

Since he had already eaten his dinner in town, he put on a pot of coffee and, when it had perked, sat looking off into the night, drinking coffee and working over in his mind the possible destinations the killers might have in mind.

East, the direction in which the men seemed to be heading, lay only two small homesteads. There was Fred Simms's place. Simms was a small-time sheep rancher. And there was Hap Hinkle's outfit.

Cooper weighed which would be the most likely choice. Fred Simms was an ornery old bastard, and he and his dozen dogs would not be an easy mark for anyone.

Hinkle was still a mystery. The old man was something of a legend, and Cooper had

37

met him only once. Hinkle was reputed to be one of the most successful highwaymen of all time, though no one had ever garnered enough evidence for prosecution. It was alleged that many years ago Harold "Hap" Hinkle had robbed stages to the tune of over thirty thousand dollars in gold and currency. And no lawman had even come close to tying him in to any robberies.

There had been a romantic aura about Hinkle as a young man in the prime of his cunning and daring. He had never injured anyone in his holdups. As Cooper had heard the story, the bandit had been especially courteous and respectful of women passengers, calming their fears, seeing that they were neither discomforted or inconvenienced beyond being lightened of their burden of wealth.

Hinkle had worked mainly the Pacific Northwest: Oregon, Idaho, and Washington territories, with an occasional excursion up into British Columbia.

Insofar as Marshal Ben Cooper was aware, there were no federal warrants on the man — at least no current ones — indicating that the old bandit had, quite likely, retired and had taken up a respectable, law-abiding lifestyle. A little prospecting, he had explained to the marshal.

On the occasion of that one meeting, Cooper

remembered, there had been a young girl — Hinkle's niece or daughter, it was never explained which. The two had come into town for supplies that had not been available at Sinclair's store. The girl had ridden a pregnant mare, Cooper recalled, a good-looking paint.

Their conversation with the marshal had been limited, their answers to his questions respectful but short. They had stayed in town no more than an hour, and they had ridden out the way they had come in, disappearing like dust devils in the shimmering desert heat. That meeting had been nearly a year ago.

The fire had burned low when Cooper rolled in his blanket. The steeldust stood close by, ground-tied. The last thing Cooper did before closing his eyes was to pull his six-gun from its holster and lay it beneath the blanket, close to hand.

By far the worst thing for anyone following another's trail happened to Cooper in the middle of the night. It began with a light thumping on the canvas tarp covering his bedroll and ended in a steady downpour that increased enough in volume to create a narrow rushing stream in the bottom of the creek bed below his camp.

Wisely he had chosen for his spot to bed down an area that was safe from being washed away. He got up long enough to scoop a narrow ditch around his bed to carry off the water, and then crawled back under the tarp, checking to be sure that his six-gun was close and dry.

The rain quit and dawn broke at almost the same time, and except for slightly damp bedding, nothing and no one was the worse for wear.

Cooper spent the next hour drying his gear, spreading the blankets over the large boulders, and eating breakfast.

When he was in the saddle, he knew before looking that the trail left by the four killers had been washed out of existence. Had the quarry been close ahead, he might have circled wide in an effort to pick up a fresh trail. This move, he realized, was hopeless. They were too far ahead, leaving him to rely on common sense and his ability to read the killers' minds.

There was a spring Cooper knew of, located about seven miles due east from where he stood. It was not inconceivable that the four might make a rest stop at the water hole through the heat of the day and then continue on to Hinkle's place.

He rode slowly into the morning sun, oblivious to the splendid display of golden rays touching off fire and colored lights in the sandstone buttes and rocky slopes behind him. It was a country teeming with game: small desert deer, coyotes, rodents, and rattlesnakes, each especially suited for life on the harsh, unforgiving desert.

By midmorning the sky turned brassy yellow, straining the eye and making the sweat run down his back beneath his shirt, soaking the girth strap of the steeldust.

A broad-winged shadow flitted across the rough ground below the horse's plodding nose. Cooper looked up at a hawk that banked and glided effortlessly on the rising heatwaves.

Shortly before midday he reached the water hole. To someone unaware of its existence it was a pile of boulders beneath a massive butte. Between the boulders was a deep basin in solid rock, fed by rainwater and protected from the sun by the butte itself. And it was always cold and satisfying to the body and spirit of the hot and weary traveler.

Cooper lay full length on the rock shelf and drank his fill. When the horse had watered, he remounted and circled the area. He found an indication of hoofprints, sloughed over by the night's rain, but once away from the protection of the butte they quickly played out. The combined effort of wind and rain had erased all sign of the four horsemen's passing.

The marshal was comforted and at the same time worried. The short distance he had been able to follow the tracks convinced him the four were making for the Hinkle place. He found himself hoping as he rode that the old robber would prove as wily dealing with the four killers as when dodging the law.

He pressed on through the heat of the day and rode up to the adobe house when the sun was well into its decline. At least he found where the house had stood. There lay there now a jumbled pile of broken adobe bricks, splinters of wood and dust, a few tools, an occasional leg of furniture. There was virtually nothing recognizable left of the structure itself.

He dismounted solemnly and wandered through the wreckage. The smell of cordite was strong. Dynamite. It was as though a huge fist had smashed the building flat.

When he was satisfied there were no bodies buried beneath the rubble, he turned his attention to the confused tangle of tracks. Though the rain had done its best, the ground was more porous around the house, and a welter of smudged prints remained.

Squatting on his haunches he sorted out the boot prints of four men, a set of moccasin prints, and the impressions of small bare feet.

In number that would account for Hinkle and the girl and the four killers, the one still wearing the Indian footgear.

South of where the house had stood was

a small corral with a wooden shelter at one end. Cooper blinked. A small brown-and-white paint foal was staring at him, confused and fearful, through the poles of the corral. It whinnied softly, dashed off and ran a quick circle, then returned to take up again staring at the stranger.

The foal was too young to be on its own without the mare. A little alarm went off in the back of Cooper's brain.

He walked slowly in the direction of the foal, loosening his gun in the holster. There were tracks and hoofprints aplenty in the area of the corral, but none seemed fresh. Yet he approached the shed warily.

The steeldust whickered softly at his elbow. Cooper glanced at the horse and saw its attention focused on the back side of the shed. A shallow gully encircled the corral on the south side. Moving a few more cautious steps forward, Cooper spotted the remains of a small fire in the bottom of the wash.

At the corral's northwest corner he eased over the lip of the gully and moved up on the hidden back side of the shed, hand resting on the butt of his six-gun.

When he rounded the corner of the building, he came to a sudden and abrupt stop. His first thought was a prayer that the child had not been made to watch. It was butchery, performed slowly and methodically. Cooper imagined he could hear the dying man's screams echoing back from the buttes.

Hinkle's eyelids had been cut away, laying his naked eyes helplessly exposed to the sun. That was likely the first thing done. The rest was an unspeakable orgy of cruelty, performed with knives, whip, and fire.

Cooper sat down on the sandy bottom of the gully. He bowed his head and rubbed his eyes. His breathing was an effort.

It took several minutes for the marshal to muster the will to push himself to his feet. He had to find out the fate of the child and go on. And that demanded first a search of the area.

It took only a brief search to determine that the girl, dead or alive, was not there. They had taken her. Cooper's heart felt like lead. He almost wished, as he searched, that he might find her body. At least her misery would have been at an end. Now, he didn't want to think of the hell she must, maybe even at this moment, be facing.

Cooper fought back a sense of futility. For the girl's sake he must remain hopeful, and he must use every ounce of his energy and savvy to hunt down the bastards who had taken her. Whether she lived or died, he vowed, the four would be found.

The first order of business lay in the burying of the old man. He found a shovel blade in the rubble and, though the handle was missing, he was able to scoop a trench in the sand behind where the house had stood.

He had nothing with which to wrap the old man. The best he could manage was to unknot his own bandana and lay it over the scarcely recognizable face before filling in the grave and covering the mound with a shell of loose rocks.

The steeldust stood back a ways, watching the procedure. When Cooper finished, he wiped the sweat from his face on his shirt-sleeves and contemplated the big animal.

"We got a big job ahead of us now, pardner."

The horse flicked his ears in response.

It was too late in the day to make much progress tracking, but Cooper couldn't bring himself to spend the night in this place. He resolved to avail himself of Fred Simms's crusty hospitality and have, perhaps, his last full meal for some time. Besides, he had to do something with the foal. He just couldn't leave the little horse to die out here. And if, by some miracle, he was able to rescue the girl, he would like to be able to at least tell her that her little horse was safe.

He took his rope from his saddle, walked

over to the corral, and slipped through the poles of the fence.

The foal bolted to the far end of the pen. Cooper saw that it was a little filly with wide-set, innocent eyes that flashed with spirit and fear. It was clear the little horse had had enough of mankind for a time.

He worked out a wide Hoolihan loop in the lariat and advanced on the foal, dragging the loop in the dust behind him.

He missed the first toss, the rope hanging up ever so briefly on the little white rump. It took several minutes of soothing talk to calm the animal enough for a second try.

This time the loop settled neatly about the graceful little neck; there was only token resistance after that. Once the filly felt Cooper's kind hands her most violent fears seemed allayed. In fact, she seemed, after a few minutes, almost grateful for the reassuring contact.

When the little horse was standing quiet, Cooper pushed a second loop of the rope up under the first loop about the neck, slipped the second loop across the tender muzzle, and tightened it gently, forming a makeshift halter.

There were no further problems after that — Hinkle or the girl had done one hell of a fine job of halter-breaking the filly, and she followed along docilely beside the marshal and the steeldust.

46

It was after dark when they reached Simms's place. At the marshal's hail, a long black barrel poked through one glass-less window.

"You might be the marshal," came the gravel-voiced challenge, "and then again, maybe not. If it turns out you ain't, you'll likely end up with a hole in yer innards you can stuff yer hat through."

All this was said above the din of barking dogs. The filly danced nervously on the end of the rope.

"Quiet them goddamn dogs down so we can talk," Cooper ordered. "I got a little horse here and they're scaring the hell out of her."

The note of authority in the marshal's voice seemed to convince Simms. He lighted a lamp, quieted the dogs, and slowly opened the door.

"I'm on the trail of four men," Cooper explained in a more congenial tone. "Anyone ride by?"

"I ain't seen no one," Simms growled. "I mind my own business and I 'spect others to do the same."

"Yeah. That's all well and good. But for a while you're going to be mindin' a little of my business. If I got it figured right, this little critter here belongs to Hap Hinkle's kid. I'm leavin' her with you until I get the girl back."

"Get the girl back? What the hell you talkin' 'bout, Marshal?"

"Well," Cooper replied sarcastically. "I'm real pleased you invited me. Be right glad for some supper and a cup of nice hot coffee."

The darkened silhouette was silent a moment. "All right. All right. Haul yer butt inside here. I got a little slumgullion left. Take care of yer horses later."

"I'll take care of the horses now," Cooper replied. "You be sure that coffee's hot."

He moved off from the lamp's glow toward the vague outline of a corral and livestock sheds. He put the foal in with the steeldust, reassured by the soft whickering from the little horse that placing her in with an older, comforting presence was the right move.

He forked hay for both horses into the mangers and filled the grain boxes with oats from a wooden-staved barrel.

"I ain't runnin' a hotel here," growled Simms, "but I still expect to be paid for my troubles."

Cooper looked around the cluttered room. A pair of mule-ear-flapped boots lay on the floor by a single bunk bed. Firewood, mostly sage and greasewood, was piled in a corner by the stove. No curtains, no pictures, only the essentials of existence.

A dog-eared, frayed Montgomery Ward catalog lay open on the floor beside the boots. The exposed pages displayed illustrated drawings of young women posed in corsets and undergarments.

"Yeah," Cooper said, throwing his saddle on the floor. "I can see you went to a lot of trouble." He stood his Winchester in a corner near the saddle. He took a cup that looked reasonably clean from a shelf by the stove and filled it with the somber black brew from the enameled pot.

He took a cautious sip and grimaced.

"Don't worry, Simms. You'll be paid. Federal government always pays its bills. Sooner or later. Dish me up some of that slop, will you?"

"What d'ya mean, sooner or later?" Simms demanded. "I'm talkin' right now."

"Right now," Cooper answered wearily, "what you get is a voucher. You bring it in next time you're in town. You and me, we go over to the bank and get your money. End of discussion on that matter. I'll be having that stew now."

Simms's jaws worked helplessly as he watched Cooper drop lazily onto the one chair in the room.

He answered the marshal's questioning stare with a growl, turned to the stove, and filled a shallow bowl from a large covered cook pot.

"It ain't right," he muttered, handing the bowl to Cooper and stalking over to the bunk.

49

"Man builds hisself a home. 'Nother man marches in an' takes over. All in the name of Lord High Government!"

"It's all a part of the way this great free land of ours works," mimicked Cooper. He attacked the stew without reservation. He actually didn't want to know what the stew was comprised of; many men, living by themselves in tight circumstances, often fell to eating things that lived on the lower end of the food chain. Among some men rattlesnake was considered prime, or a desert rat, salamander stew. . . . Cooper shoveled it in, not failing to catch the humorous glint in the eyes of Simms, who was sitting on the edge of the bunk watching him.

"S'pose you'll be awantin' my bunk next?"

Cooper looked at the tangle of matted blankets, visualizing all manner of vermin within the rank folds.

"I found a sweet mow of hay out in the shed. I'll throw my roll out there. Thanks just the same."

He placed his empty coffee cup — a refill had not been necessary — next to his empty bowl and pushed wearily to his feet.

"I'll likely be gone 'fore you're awake, Simms. Like I said, you get to town and we'll settle up." Cooper looked deep into the old man's eyes. "You're to take care of that filly,

50

you hear? She's to be kept in the prime of health. Four men took the little gal what owns that horse. I'll be getting her back. And when I do, she'll be wanting her horse."

Cooper closed the door softly behind him, leaving Simms weighing the character of Marshal Ben Cooper against that of the creature whose remains comprised the essence of the slumgullion that evening.

CHAPTER 7

There were five of them now. The girl rode the paint mare, and only the old man, Deke Chambers, noticed the hard set to her jaw, the unwavering blue eyes fixed on the trail ahead. The girl had strength. That could be dangerous.

He had shown — and it surprised even him — a trace of compassion by not insisting she watch their efforts with Hinkle. But Hinkle had screamed — lord, how he had screamed — and she had sure heard the screams.

It was afterward, when they were mounted, ready to ride, that he had noticed the hard glint in the girl's tear-reddened eyes. He saw that she was frightened — unto death itself — but she could move and she could act. He noticed she had scarcely flinched when the dynamite tore into dust and kindling what had been her home. It was at that point that Deke knew the child would bear watching.

They rode in single file, the bravura and swagger gone. Each rode alone with his own dismal thoughts. They had failed with the old man. Though he had screamed his heart out, he had died without telling the location of the money.

Their trail led east, over hardpan, leaving little trace of their passing. The weather had cooled somewhat, and the sun, a brassy, glaring ball, shone as though through cheesecloth. There was a haze that distorted distances. The air had lost its purity and settled in the lungs like air pulled through a dirty blanket.

"You think the girl would know?" asked Delwin Chambers, the bearded one with the whip. The whip hung from his saddle and he stroked its leather coils as he rode.

His father looked at him with disgust. "We give her a chance to tell. We ast her. If she knew, you think she would've kept still whilst ol' Hap be screamin' his head off?"

Though the girl rode between them, they spoke as though she were not there.

"I don't know," put in little Frankie Chambers from behind. "Lot of folks are pretty brave when it's someone else doin' the hurtin'."

"Maybe a taste o' the wild wind'll loosen her tongue," Delwin said, looking at the girl and licking his lips.

The girl gave him a brittle stare.

"Hap never kept none of that money," she

said without wavering. "I can't tell you where it is if it don't exist."

"That's what you say now, little sister," declared Frankie. "But I know fer a fact the old man took more'n thirty thousand dollars offen them stages. What did he do, lose it?"

She turned in the saddle. "It went out like it came in — easy. You think we'd be livin' in the cabin if Hap had that much money?"

The old man gave the girl a sidelong glance. She was scared, but she wasn't going to show it. Deke admired that. And it was sounding more and more likely that she was telling the truth. Grudgingly he was coming to the conclusion that there might not be any money to be had, that Hap Hinkle had indeed spent all he took from the robberies.

He smiled philosophically. It had been worth a try. Nothing lost. Additionally, they had the girl, whatever that was worth. Deke Chambers felt no remorse for the human beings left dead in their wake. Some things had to be, that was all. Deke Chambers needed money and lots of it, and if the price had to be paid in a few human lives, so be it.

"Gal's got a point, Frankie," he told his youngest son. "I think we been on a wild goose chase."

Lance Chambers, riding in front, spoke low, over his shoulder. "If that be the case,

54

Pa, I think we owe Mr. Dekker something fer that fake information. We wasted all this time, wore out ourselves and our horses fer nothin'." He scratched his scraggly chin and spat disgustedly at a small green lizard sunning on a rock.

Delwin chuckled. "Big brother, you be much too trustin' to begin with. I figured ol' Dekker just be yarnin' anyway."

Lance turned on him. "You're a great one for hindsight. Why the hell didn't you say somethin' or do somethin' when we still had the chance? Someone should shut the bastard's lying mouth."

"I don't think we be hearin' much more from Mr. Dekker, Lance boy," said the father. He smiled. "Be that right, Delwin?"

"Pert near right, Pa." Delwin pulled a silver watch case from his pocket.

Lance recognized the timepiece as one he had seen in Dekker's possession.

Lance turned his eyes back to the trail. "That still leaves us the problem of the girl," he muttered to no one in particular.

"At this point," replied his father, "she be no particular problem. If we be called upon to move swiftly, she may then become an inconvenience."

"So far there's only one on the trail," said Frankie. "And he's many miles back.

55

The hardpan's slowin' him up."

"He better hope he don't get too damn close," said Delwin with a savage twist to his mouth. "He'll be feelin' the ol' wild wind whippin' up his backside."

At that, Frankie broke into laughter. "Maybe that little gal beside you there would like a little breeze from that old wind Del. Might take that sour look offen her face."

Lance pulled his horse up and turned in the saddle. "You be leavin' the girl alone. Skinnin' the old man was one thing. Pullin' yer tricks on the gal is somethin' else. I ain't goin' to abide it."

Delwin was on the point of a reply when he noticed the hard glint in his brother's eye. "Makes no never mind to me," he said. "Frankie's idea, not mine."

"But it's yer whip," said Lance flatly.

"Lance is right," interjected the father, kicking his own horse and starting the small caravan again on its way. "That gal ever needs skinnin', I'll do it. Remember that, all three of you. We may just need her fer ransom or such. An' I don't want her marked up just yet."

Before he turned away, Christie had one instant of eye contact with Lance. She hoped that her impression had been correct, that she had read a true compassion in those eyes. His were the first words spoken in her defense since Hap had pleaded with them to set her free.

As concerned as Christie was for her own safety, the girl's heart ached at the thought of the foal she had been forced to leave behind, penned, languishing without food, without the mare's milk. She prayed with all her might that someone might come along and care for the little horse — if not seeing to its needs, at least putting a merciful end to its suffering.

She knew without looking that the paint mare's udder was already swollen and painful. Maybe when they stopped for the night the animal would allow her to milk off some of the pressure.

Christie would not allow herself to think of Hap. Somewhere in her brain a floodgate had been dropped, shutting off the horror. Existence for Christie had begun yesterday morning when she was forced onto the back of the paint mare to ride away with the four men. Her only tie with the past, beyond the mare, was her concern for the foal. And soon, for the sake of its own survival, her mind would shut out that little lost life too. Mercifully, the brain would allow only so much pain to enter until connections with reality were severed. For now, grief must wait. Her own survival was the issue at hand.

"Who do you figure is behind us, Pa?" asked Frankie. "You know, maybe he ain't after us at all. Maybe he's just prospectin', or a traveler or sumpin'."

His father looked at him strangely. "Be you more stupid than you look? Of course he be after us. Therefore he be the law."

"Goddamn cocksure one," put in Lance, "if it just be himself after the four of us." He stopped and turned in the saddle, straining his eyes in an effort to pick up the distant horseman. "Ain't no one back there no ways."

"Is so!" declared Frankie hotly. "Every once in a while there'll be a puff of dust."

"He's back there," affirmed the old man.

"What're we goin' to do, Pa?" Delwin asked.

"Keep going," answered the father impatiently. "Might surprise you, Del, but I don't have *everything* worked out ahead of time."

"Never would've guessed that," muttered Lance, loud enough for his own ears alone.

Deke Chambers said, "We'll just keep moving to them mountains until the wind changes, or the lawman catches up."

Christie turned slowly in the saddle, searching past Frankie's leering smile for a glimpse of the one who might rescue her from these savage men.

"Turn around, daughter," instructed the old man. "Your salvation yet be a long ways off."

The girl turned sullenly back to the trail. Her heart cried out to the lawman. Please hurry!

CHAPTER 8

Cooper found tracking across the hardpan surface tough going, even though five horses were making the trail. Before reaching the rocky surface, he had found an occasional print in the sand. Far ahead he might spot a moving dust cloud. Now, even that was gone.

There was one cause for optimism: Past tracks indicated the horsemen had lined out pretty much in a straight line. Whether because they had a definite destination in mind or had no regard for pursuit, they remained on the projected course, and Cooper could pretty much base his pursuit on probables.

There was nothing, he cautioned himself, to keep them from changing course; from changing again and again, for that matter. They were free to exercise their whims, move erratically in one direction, abruptly change to another, much like a ship tacking into a heavy headwind. But as long as their direction remained more or less true, Cooper figured he was still in the running. And so was the girl.

They were headed due east toward the San Juans, some three hundred miles in the hazy distance. The going could not help but become easier. He felt he stood a good chance of overtaking the band before they reached the Colorado border.

It was now the morning of the third day since the girl's abduction. Repeatedly Cooper forced himself to put aside thoughts of the child. He must concentrate on the pursuit, without regard to any urgency because of whatever his imagination told him she might be enduring at that moment. He could do the girl no good if he wore out himself or his horse. And he could not help her or capture the four if he rode into a trap. So his pursuit was methodical, careful, and relentless. No one could say when it would happen, but he *would* catch up to them. Then and only then would he allow himself to think about the girl.

Cooper rode relaxed, picking the easiest way for the steeldust. The gelding was an excellent horse and a tough horse. But Cooper was two hundred thirty pounds of man, plus tack and supplies. Such a burden would eventually take the starch out of any animal.

Around noon he lost all pretense of a trail and pulled up to consider. He stepped off the horse, loosened the cinch, and walked about to loosen cramped joints.

Sipping at his canteen, he squinted into the distance. Another two days, if they continued their present course, would take them past the ancient ruins at Hovenweep in the still-hostile desert and into the more comfortable higher altitudes of the slopes.

He played over in his mind possible destinations the killers might have in mind.

Directly ahead, east, northeast, he could think of only ramshackle communities, down-and-out settlements. Higher up in the mountains, unless he closed the distance sooner, they would hit the mining towns: Rico, Silverton, and, farther up, Telluride. As a federal marshal, Cooper had no jurisdictional worries. However, if the killers did strike off into the mountains, it would be wise to find a telegraph office and wire the regional marshal's office in Denver. If no help in the actual pursuit could be obtained, perhaps they would at least have some information as to the identity of Cooper's quarry.

Nightfall found him making a fireless camp at the edge of a brackish pond. The water smacked slightly of alkali, and while it served the horse's purpose, Cooper drank of the sweet water in his canteen.

There was a chill in the air when he rolled

in his blanket. A coyote cried from far away, a moment later a faint answering cry. Off to his right, somewhere among the rocks, something slithered. The steel shoe of his horse struck a stone. And then he was asleep.

CHAPTER 9

Christie lay shivering in the one thin blanket the old man had given her. Her feet were bare and she wore the tattered jeans and Navajo shirt she had worn the day of her capture. The remainder of her clothing and her boots, along with her warm coat, had been in the house when it was destroyed. In short, she was totally unprepared for the ordeal. Had not Chambers feared she might get sick and slow them up, Christie surmised miserably, she probably wouldn't even have the blanket.

Despite the old man's stern warning, she had managed an occasional glance to the rear, hoping for an encouraging sign that they were still pursued. Once, she had thought she had seen something move, but it was much too close to have been the lawman. More likely a deer or such, she reasoned.

Besides being cold, hunger gnawed at her insides. Her captors allowed her little food, perhaps because they were short themselves.

That thought, as uncomfortable as she was physically, gave her a warming hope. If they were low on supplies, they would have to seek someplace where they could get more, a town or a farm. And where there were people, she might find someone to help her.

Wrapped in their own heavy bedrolls, the four men snored comfortably around her. They had placed their beds in a square, with her own in the middle. Beneath her own blanket, around one slim ankle, Delwin had tied a rawhide tether. The other end was fastened to his left wrist. She had nearly smiled at that. If she took it in mind to escape, it would take more than a little piece of rawhide to hold her back.

With a sagacity beyond her years, Christie realized that for now it was not just a question of escaping their clutches, but of having someplace or someone to run to. Like as not, if it came to making a run for it, she would get only one chance, and she knew she must weigh her opportunities carefully.

As she lay staring up into the vast smear of stars, it came to her with a sad little jolt the change in her life, wrought in only two days' time.

Only last week Hap had talked positively of putting her in a girls' school in Denver. It had sounded wondrous, dreamlike. There,

Hap had promised, she would wear pretty dresses, fine leather shoes, and her hair would be curled and arranged in the manner of fine ladies.

Christie had nearly wept with delight. But how, she had wondered after some reflection, would Hap Hinkle, grizzled and woolly, take to city living?

"Ah hell, sweet pea," he had said, looking dismayed, when she raised the question. "I ain't goin' with ya. What would an old buzzard like me do in the city?"

She had looked alarmed, frightened.

"No, no. It's all right," he quickly assured her. "My sister lives in Denver. You'll be livin' at the school, but you can visit Ruthie anytime you want. An' you'll get along with her just fine. She's damn near as ornery as me."

That arrangement could work. Christie felt she could accept those terms and thrive easily enough. Though she would miss Hap, of course.

Boarding school, his sister — Hap had done considerable thinking on this idea. With all the promised glitter of the new life, clothes and an education, Christie's grasp of reality again asserted itself.

"Hap," she had asked. "Where the hell we goin' to get all that money? We don't have no money for that kind of foofaraw." As if to emphasize her point she glanced down at her roughed-out men's work shoes, which she chanced to be wearing that day to protect a cactus-punctured big toe.

"That's my worry, prune cake." And he had smiled strangely. "When you need it, the money will be there for ya. 'Member our secret, doncha? One I told you about when you were just a mite?"

Now she shivered and pulled the flimsy blanket close around her throat. How she longed for sleep, a few hours' escape from her misery.

Delwin groaned in his sleep, and Christie felt a sharp tug on her ankle binding. Of the four, she feared Delwin the most. Her fear went beyond his ragged, delirious joy at using his whip. When they rode she felt his eyes upon her. Through all this long day, the third since her capture, she had felt a growing self-consciousness of her young-womanhood — her rounding hips and her budding bosoms pressing against the confines of the thin Navajo shirt.

Lance, surly and taciturn, seemed to Christie the least threatening. If she were to hope for mercy from any one of them, it would be from this craggy, worn-looking man.

Frankie was different, truly different.

Christie noticed right off the small hands with pointed fingernails, his delicate voice, and off-hand way of stating something serious, his effeminate, mincing steps in the beaded moccasins. The face was soft and what beard there was, was soft and scraggly. But the feminine softness was lost in the cruel eyes.

In Papa Deke Chambers Christie sensed the root of the family's evil nature. He was the rock, the foundation of their acts of terror.

When she at last dropped off to sleep, it was with her heart held in the cold grip of these four terrible men, and the cold, unforgiving night to which they had committed her soul.

Awareness returned when her ankle was jerked sharply from under the blanket by the rawhide tether.

"Up an' at 'em, missy." Delwin grinned. "You want any breakfast, you best be gettin' a fire goin'."

It was cold, gray dawn. Deke Chambers allowed a smokeless fire early in the morning and at no other time — never at night when the fire's glare might be seen.

Groggily, Christie reached down to untie the rawhide.

"I'll take care of that." Delwin dropped to his knees and made a point of holding her small foot in his hand while he fumbled overly long with the knot.

When he released her, Christie withdrew her foot, feeling disgusted as though she'd stepped in something foul.

Delwin smiled lopsidedly, his yellow-flecked eyes probing into hers.

She looked away and scrambled to her feet, eager to be away from him.

When she got to her feet, she saw Lance seated on a large rock, appraising the situation.

Their eyes met and hers filled instantly with challenge, silently imploring him to do the manly thing and protect her from his wretched family.

His eyes wavered and then dropped back to the six-gun he was cleaning.

"I'm going to scout around, Pa," he said, rising suddenly. He moved stiffly to where the horses were tethered, selected his own, and began readying him for the trail. When Lance rode from camp, Christie was returning with an armload of wood for the fire. He rode past without a glance.

Lance returned in an hour, a worried look on his face. He dropped by the fire, poured a cup of coffee, and accepted a tin plate of griddle cakes with a few chunks of side bacon. He inspected the food a moment and then passed the plate back to Christie.

"I ain't hungry," he explained gruffly.

Christie accepted the food without comment, though she allowed a brief flash of gratitude in her eyes.

"What ails you, boy?" asked Deke Chambers. "You look like you swallowed something sideways."

Lance tasted the coffee and grimaced. "I don't know. Somethin' ain't right. I couldn't spot nothin' back there."

"You mean, brother dear," said Frankie, "we lost our shadow?" He reclined against his saddle, smoking.

Lance shook his head. "I said I don't know. But that be givin' up awful goddamn easy." He stood up and dumped his coffee on the ground.

The old man nodded thoughtfully. "I think you be right, Lance boy. If that lawman turns back this soon, he has no heart at all."

Lance approached the old man. "I be usin' your spyglass, Pa," he said.

"In my saddlebag, boy. An' you be givin' our back trail a real good going over."

Christie watched Lance ride again from the camp. Her heart sank. If the lawman should give up the chase, her chances were almost nil. The bitter possibility destroyed her enthusiastic attack on the griddle cakes, but she forced herself to eat. She would need her strength, whatever chance for survival came her way.

She was gathering up the tin plates, moving about the fire, when Delwin grabbed her. He clutched her bare ankle, jerked her off balance so that she fell on his lap, scattering the plates and utensils. She fought to pull free, to get to her feet, but he held her close and she shrank from his foul breath and bearded face.

With large frightened eyes she looked first to the old man and then to Frankie for help but found only amused grins.

"Now you just sit here a spell, missy," Delwin soothed. "It ain't goin' to hurt you none."

His arms were bands of steel. The harder she struggled, the tighter they crushed her to his chest. At last, accepting the futility of it, she lay still.

"Please let me go," she begged in an anguished whisper.

He relaxed his grip a bit. "You just sit easy awhile, gal. Rest them bones."

She noted with disgust small bits of griddle cake captured in his dark beard like flies in a spider web.

"Pa, I got me a idea," Delwin said with a happy grin. "I think I be marryin' this gal." He gave Christie a squeeze.

Deke Chambers shook his head slowly,

smiling. "I don't know now, Delwin. She be a might on the young side. Not fully bloomed yet. How old be ye, missy?"

"Eleven." Christie faltered a lie.

"I'd guess closer to fourteen — fifteen," said Frankie. "Hell, Delwin. She be old enough. Back home they marry 'em at thirteen. She be at least that old. Ain't that true now, missy?"

"What be yer name, missy?" Delwin asked. "Hell, Pa, I don't even know my wife-to-be's name. What be yer name, I say?"

The mute terror in Christie's eyes seemed to spark Delwin's new fire. It had begun as a game, but now her closeness stoked his animal lust.

"Answer yer man!" he shouted suddenly.

"Christie," she whispered. "My name's Christine Hinkle." She could not keep her lips from trembling, and she felt as though she were going to be sick. She could taste the rancid side meat in her mouth.

"That ol' man be yer pa, then?" said Deke Chambers.

The girl shook her head dumbly.

"Answer up, gal!" he ordered sharply.

"My real pa's dead," she said weakly. "Hap took me in when I was real small. Don't remember my own folks."

He eyed her speculatively. "You lived

around that old man all this time. I still can't believe he never said nothin' to you about money. Think hard, girl. We get that money and you be set free. That be my sacred promise."

Christie swallowed hard. Her mind and tongue refused to work. Papa Deke saw the terrified glance she directed at Delwin. "Turn her loose, boy," he ordered. "Can't you see you be scarin' her? The fun's over."

Christie felt Delwin's arms tighten about her.

"I said, turn her loose."

It was a whispered command, and it struck Delwin like a gunshot in his midsection. His arms dropped and Christie sprang free.

She scrambled to her feet like a startled deer, quickly skirting the fire so that it burned between her and the flush-faced Delwin.

"You think real careful now, Christie." The old man's voice poured like warm syrup. "We be talkin' about your freedom now."

"I don't remember Hap ever sayin' nothin'. Honest. I don't think he had no money." It all came in an anguished rush. "Honest, Mister Chambers."

"You call me Pa, like my boys do," he said gently. "Without that money, Christie, I might just give sway to Delwin's wish. Then you be my daughter. So you just start callin' me Papa. Get used to the sound."

Christie turned away with an inarticulate groan and began slowly picking up the scattered tin plates, all the time keeping a wary eye on Delwin.

She was kneeling, scrubbing the plates with handfuls of fine sand, when Lance returned. His course took him close to the girl, but he walked his horse past, eyes straight ahead.

The old man, Delwin, and Frankie had roused themselves, and they looked up questioningly as Lance rode up.

"You got news, boy?"

Lance dismounted. He shook his head. "I still can't see nothin'. I picked up some gunshots a long ways back."

The old man pulled his cinch strap tight with a savage jerk, then paused, reflecting.

"Could be our old lawdog got hisself into some trouble he warn't figurin' on." He smiled, exposing yellowed and decayed teeth.

"Well, Lance boy, as they say, there's no ill rain but what it don't fall on somebody's corn — or somethin' like that."

He swung atop his horse, and his sons followed his lead.

"All right, missy. Get them dishes put away an' get aboard that crowbait mare. An' I reckon you won't be havin' to work a creak in yer neck lookin' over yer shoulder anymore. I got me a good strong gut feelin' our lawman friend done give up the chase."

If you piece such a river up, and it didn't work out,
I got me a good thing going right; I can afford to
bend those things up the other way.

CHAPTER 10

Cooper awoke as the sky in the east above the mountains was tinged with the first faint smudge of gray. The soft nicker of the steeldust had roused him. He lay for a moment, eyes closed, listening. The horse had moved in close to the man, indicating, perhaps, that it had sensed some threat among the rocks and clumps of sage.

His right hand closed on his Colt. From off to his left he caught the sound of a soft, leathery scrape. And that was all.

He flung back the bedroll and rolled to his right.

The first Indian was less than a dozen feet away, upraised, long knife at the ready. From his knees, Cooper fired. The slug took the Indian square in the chest, knocking him flat on his back like a blow from a huge fist.

They seemed to spring from everywhere then, dark, menacing forms in the gray light.

Cooper swung to his right, fired, and dropped a second Indian.

76

Two, three, four charged him at once, rising from their cover like disembodied spirits. He fired into the face of the nearest. The Indian uttered a shriek, clapped his hands to his face where his jaw had been, and collapsed, falling into Cooper and knocking him flat.

Before he could regain his balance, another one was upon him. The Indian had launched himself from several feet out. He struck Cooper full in the chest as the marshal was attempting to get his feet under him.

The Indian was big and powerful, exuding the smell of the earth, sweat, and campfires. Only by exerting all his strength could Cooper keep the long knife from his throat.

He tried to maneuver his six-gun into position, but steel-banded fingers gripped his wrist and held the weapon useless to one side.

They rolled and tumbled. Cooper was aware of mocassined feet.

With one desperate effort he tore free from the savage grasp, placed a foot in the Indian's midsection, and shoved. The savage fell back, started up again, and Cooper put a bullet between the black eyes.

At the same instant he pressed the trigger, something struck his back between the shoulder blades, pushing him forward into the sand. Pain rocketed down his spine, and for a moment he was unable to draw a breath.

Instinct made him ignore the pain and shock and roll over, face up.

The Indian standing above bore a surprised look on his painted face. But only for an instant. Cooper's next slug disassembled that face.

There were more. He raised his six-gun and fired at the nearest shadow. The Indian dropped flat behind a boulder a split second before Cooper's gun bucked in his hand; the bullet went howling off into the gray dawn.

Cooper spotted another running form several yards distant and pulled the trigger once more. A dry click.

He holstered the six-gun and snatched his Winchester from the saddle where it lay on the ground next to his bedroll.

By the time he had jacked a shell into the chamber, the moving forms had vanished as so much morning mist.

He was kneeling, rifle in hand, breath coming in ragged gasps. He tried to watch everywhere, behind, ahead into the gloom. He knew he was exposed, vulnerable. He could feel the blood coursing down his back. And he felt weak, so very weak.

Did he imagine a sound behind him? The silence, so abrupt, was unnerving.

Dropping to his stomach and using the rifle butt to dig in and pull himself along, Cooper dragged himself from the open into a cluster of small boulders that gave him at least partial cover.

Peering carefully about, lest one stray bullet or arrow put an end to his incredible luck, he searched for his horse. The steeldust was gone, either grabbed by the Indians or run off by the gunfire.

He winced at the pain in his back, numb at first but now coming to life in a savage way. If he didn't do something to staunch the blood flow, he wouldn't be needing a horse.

He fired a perfunctory couple of rounds into the shadows of boulders and clumps of mesquite, then laid his rifle aside but close to hand. He was having considerable trouble controlling his right hand. With his left he unknotted his bandana from around his neck, unbuttoned his shirt, and stuffed in the cloth over his shoulder, positioning it, he hoped, onto the wound.

He had no way of knowing if it would do any good, but he had to do something. The wound was serious — how serious would be determined within the next few hours, if he survived at all.

With that strange phenomenon that sometimes comes with blood loss, he was amazingly clearheaded. It seemed he could suddenly see remarkably well through the gloom of dawn.

An arm moved behind a bush. Cooper estimated the approximate relationship of the chest that went with that arm, aimed, and squeezed off a shot.

The bush trembled and then was still.

Occasionally a shot would be fired from some place of concealment, a puff of drifting smoke indicating a bush, a mound of crusted earth, or a cluster of rocks, but no further human targets showed themselves.

An hour passed. Full daylight arrived, with Cooper firing intermittently, more to warn the enemy to keep their distance than with any actual hope of hitting anything.

He wasn't sure how he knew they had gone. He had seen no one, had heard no one ride away. He only knew, of a sudden, he was alone.

His relief was guarded. He was alone, wounded, without a horse, a good seventy-five miles from the nearest town, which would be . . . which would . . . He was growing light-headed. It was an effort to think.

He eased himself upright and rested against a rock, taking care not to disturb the wound. It felt as if the back of his shirt had dried somewhat, indicating maybe that the blood flow was coagulating. Had he a horse, he might just have a chance. Without one, it was damn hopeless.

As if sprung from his wishes, he heard a soft nicker and the click of steel against rock.

He turned swiftly, fearing first a return of his attackers. Instead of Indians, the steeldust stood, picket rope dragging, eyes wide, ears pointed and alert.

Cooper laughed softly. The horse took a few hesitant steps forward, shied at a lifeless body. He sniffed a limp, moccasined foot, stepped wide, and advanced to where the marshal sat on the ground.

"You're a brave old bugger, ain't ya?" Cooper asked, reaching up and stroking the inquiring muzzle. "Shooting starts, you hightail it. I thought we was partners."

The horse snorted, spraying Cooper's upturned face.

"Yeah. You're right," Cooper said gently. "Better to make a good run than a poor stand anyday."

He reached out a hand, grabbed the dangling tether rope, and pushing with the rifle, raised himself to his feet.

The rocks and brush and the distant mountains began to whirl. He felt his gorge rise in his throat, and he wrapped his arms about the horse's neck and clung there, swooning.

It was several minutes before he felt steady enough to try saddling the steeldust. Lifting the saddle was the roughest part, and when it was in place, something warm and wet was again flowing down his back.

Before mounting, he carefully reloaded his weapons. While fumbling through his saddlebags, he found an empty cloth flour sack that he stuffed beneath his shirt, hoping that he could again stem the flow of blood.

When at last he felt he was steady enough to mount, he gathered the reins in his left hand, placed his left foot in the stirrup, and paused a moment, working up volition for the effort.

"All right, Doc, stand good and still. You move and I'll feed you to them Indians out there."

He pulled himself up, swung his leg over the cantle, settled in the saddle, and fainted.

CHAPTER 11

Cooper had only the faintest sensation of the horse moving under him. He was far beneath the level of concern, responding only to the instinct to hang on and stay in the saddle.

He had no notion of how long he was out. When he awoke, the sun was beating down on his back, and he felt cold, very cold. Yet, where his cheek rested gainst the horse's neck he was sweating.

The first thing that caught his concern when he opened his eyes was the dangling reins, one broken off short, stepped on by his steeldust. He clutched the saddle horn, and the horse continued to amble forward, skirting large boulders, edging its way around the clumps of mesquite and greasewood.

Cooper had no choice in his near-delirious condition but to let the horse have its way. He continued to lose consciousness, drifting in and out at short intervals. He felt the chances were good the horse would head for people, or at least water, which might eventually lead to the former.

At one point, early in the afternoon, he guessed, he roused himself enough to see that the horse had carried him to the lip of a low hill below which lay a shallow valley. He saw the row of trees down the center of the otherwise arid ground and gave an exultant sigh. Trees never grow in a row like that unless along the banks of a waterway. He was now to the stage where he craved water terribly. Whether awake or unconscious, his feverish body cried out for moisture.

"Congratulations are in order, Doc," he croaked to the horse as they started down the slope. "Just get me to that water, boy," he urged, slumped over the horse's neck, "and you get the night off with pay."

On a strip of rocky talus the horse slipped and abruptly sat down, nearly unseating the marshal. Cooper groaned and held to the saddle horn with whitened knuckles. He fought to hang on to consciousness, biting the inside of his cheek until he tasted blood, ramming his feet hard into the stirrups.

The steeldust managed to get his legs back under him and regain a semblance of footing. They reached the bottom without further incident.

Once on the valley floor, the line of trees seemed an incredibly long ways off. Horse and rider moved slowly across the rough terrain, the horse wending its careful way, seeming to sense the delicate condition of its burden.

Before they reached the trees, Cooper fainted again. He had known, after the jolt he had taken when the horse slipped, that his wound had reopened for the second time. Fight as he may, he could not keep his remaining strength from slipping away.

This time his head lolled sideways, down toward the stirrup. His fingers lost their grip on the saddle horn, and he tumbled to the ground, tangled in a blanket of darkness.

Later, much later, through a thick haze, he became aware of soft yet strong hands helping him back into the saddle. Through his delirium he heard voices, one softly feminine, and another, young, strident, inquisitive.

He was aware of motion, of lamplight, of floating through the pages of a picturebook filled with brightly colored braided rugs, pictures in softly glowing walnut frames, pictures of stern-looking men and women in formal clothing. He floated above a finely quilted bedspread, embroidered pillowcases, and dived, at long last, into the incredible sweet coolness of sheets.

Throughout the night his body was assaulted first by raging temperatures followed by chills so violent that he shook. He could hear moans from far off — someone needing his help. When he tried to rise to go to the aid of the one crying out, gentle hands pressed him back. The moaning grew closer, and at last he realized it was coming from his own lips.

At times the whispered voices were almost clear; a child, most certainly, and a woman. Of no importance — of no importance at all.

Occasionally something warm and wet was forced between his lips. His forehead was constantly bathed in coolness.

All in all, the dream was not unpleasant. Toward morning it began to fade, and he felt himself rising, close enough to it to reach out and grip reality.

The reality broke through with the sun, and his first lucid vision was of a papered wall, mottled by the shadows of a lilac bush outside the window.

And he was alone. And he was confused. The voices had vanished with the delirium, but still there was the air of unreality about the room, a crazy quilt of simple, hewn log walls covered with gentle finery, graceful pictures, knick-knacks fashioned from pine cones or seeds.

Cooper steeled himself and raised onto one elbow. He tried his best to ignore the pain and dizziness, but a groan escaped him nonetheless.

A blanket hanging across the doorway was pushed aside, and a young woman entered the room.

"Lay back," she ordered brusquely. "I worked too hard and went without too much sleep to get that wound starting to knit. I'll not have you tearing it open again."

It had been a dream after all. This firm, even biting voice could not be the soothing one he had heard comforting him in the night.

He obeyed and lay back with a sigh, looking up into the blackest pair of eyes he had ever seen. They were set in a triangular shaped, olive-hued face of striking beauty. An Indian, he realized, had saved his life.

A chuckle welled up from within his chest, more a crackle. What irony, what god-lovin' irony. He had just finished killing he knew not how many Indians, only to be snatched from the jaws of death by this one.

He saw the perfect black brows arch in puzzlement, watched the strong, brown hands wring a cloth in a water bucket, place it carefully on his forehead. He tried to push it away, but found, somewhat chagrined, that for the first time since he was small, a woman was stronger than he was.

He used the moment to inspect her more

closely, noting first that she wore, in place of buckskins, the long cotton dress of a white woman. Her hair, black as a crow's wing, was parted severely in the middle and held in a tight knot in the back by small silver combs. Her nose was not broad and flat, but small and sharply defined. Her lips and chin were carved of immovable stone. A smile would shatter them. Her one adornment, other than the silver combs in her hair, was a small gold locket suspended from a gold link chain about her bronzed neck.

"Your fever is down," she said stonily. "If we can keep the infection under control, I think soon you will be all right."

"I'm grateful," he said, weakly. "How's my horse?"

"He's being cared for," she answered shortly. She placed a fresh cold cloth on his forehead and straightened up. "I'll fix you something to eat. You're strong enough for some solid food now, I think."

She brushed the blanket door aside and was gone, leaving him alone with a headache and some puzzling questions.

When she returned she carried a tray with a bowl of wheat cereal and a cup of coffee. After helping him sit up and positioning the tray on his lap, she turned again to leave.

"Ma'am, if I could trouble you —"

"You have been a trouble to me, Marshal. An intolerable trouble. And I wish you to eat and regain your strength as quickly as possible so you can be on your way." She whirled and was gone, leaving Cooper staring after the swaying blanket.

He ate, slowly at first, and then finding he was ravenous, scraped the last bit of cereal from the bowl. The coffee also was delicious, and he was debating the feasibility of asking the strange woman for a second cup when she suddenly reappeared.

He asked her bluntly, "Apart from getting myself wounded, ma'am, have I done somethin' wrong that I'm not aware of?"

"You're here, Marshal, and that's enough." She scooped the bowl and coffee cup from his hand. "You're sleeping in my bed, eating my food, demanding my time. This is no hotel, Marshal."

Enough was enough. He threw the blankets aside, swung his bare legs over the side of the bed.

"If you'll hand me my clothes, ma'am, I'll trouble you no longer. Appreciate your kindness." His emphasis on the last word did not get by her.

"You're in no condition to leave," she said woodenly. "That wound will reopen before you've gone a mile."

"I guess that'll be my worry. Again I want to thank you for all your trouble. I'll give you a voucher. You can turn it in at any telegraph office. They'll give you some money for my night's lodging. Now, if you'll hand me my pants."

Looking down upon him, hunched over, wasted, unshaven, her eyes softened just a bit. "You've been here three days, Marshal," she said softly, "not one. And you need bed rest for at least another week."

"Three days?" he groaned.

She nodded, then placed a hand on his shoulder, as if to press him back down on the bed.

His face registered pain and he resisted feebly. "My God, I've lost them. They'll have reached the mountains by now." He actually rose to his feet this time, swaying uncertainly, before his knees gave way and he dropped to the bed. Gray spots floated before his eyes. He felt an electric tingle in his brain and a roaring in his ears.

When his head cleared a bit he looked up at her apologetically. "Just got up too fast, that's all."

Her stone lips worked. "I'm sorry, Marshal. I shouldn't have talked to you that way. We both know you're not able to ride. Now please lay back and be still. You're very weak yet."

He shook his head. "You don't understand. I can't. Four men captured a young girl. Killed some folks. Killed the old man she was stayin' with. God knows what she's goin' through." He rose to his feet once more, and this time stood firm, though his face turned white beneath the tanned skin.

The woman looked at him in astonishment. "Marshal, *you* don't understand. You have a four-inch stab wound in your back. I stitched it up with my sewing thread, but if you do any riding those stitches are going to pull out. You must stay. Those bandages must be changed daily."

Cooper sighed. She felt she had won until he said, "Could you help me into my clothes, ma'am?"

She spun angrily and snatched his pants and a fresh, clean man's shirt from a chair.

"You're a fool, Marshal. You'll not do that girl any good if you're dead. Besides," she fumed as she helped him into his clothes, "the chance of picking up a trail now will be impossible. We had a terrible wind night before last."

He stood, a bit embarrassed, while she buttoned the shirt.

"This is a nice shirt," he said. "I take it mine was not worth salvaging."

"It was filthy and covered with blood, just

91

as this one will soon be. I washed your pants, too. In case you hadn't noticed," she added sullenly.

"Ain't none of my business, ma'am. But how did you happen to have a man's shirt lying around?"

She pressed her lips tightly together, and for a moment Cooper thought she would not answer.

"It was my husband's," she said quietly. "He was a big man, like you."

She refused to help him strap on his gun. Throughout his unconscious period it had hung in its holster over the back of a chair next to the bed.

"Even delirious," she said, "you demanded your gun be close. I don't approve of guns, Marshal. But I realize a man in your profession must use one."

He nodded grimly, struggling with the buckle. He realized, with a jab of anxiety, that his dizziness had returned. The pulse in his head thundered like an Indian war drum, and his mouth felt dry and tingling.

He tried to fight it through. If he could just keep on his feet, it would pass, he was sure.

"What happened to your husband?"

"Dead."

"Did I dream it, or is there a child around?"

"You didn't dream it. My little boy. He's

been playing outside, to keep things quiet for you."

"I'd like to see him," Cooper said.

"Thad doesn't take much to strangers," she said simply. "He's half Ute." He saw a twinkle in her black eyes that could have been humor or sarcasm.

Something was missing. "I seem to have lost my hat in all the fuss. I hate to ask you for anything more, but you wouldn't have an old hat of your husband's lying about, would you?"

Her glittering eyes searched his face. Inscrutable, they did not show her concern over his pallid, drawn features, the fever burning again in his eyes.

She nodded. "Wait here. Rest a moment." She left the room, moving, true to her blood, as soundlessly as a spirit.

When she returned with the hat, a well-used but still serviceable Stetson, he lay on the floor by the bed.

She stared a moment, sighed, and tossed the hat on the chair.

"Thad," she called. "I need your help." And then she went resolutely about maneuvering Cooper's limp, leaden frame up onto the bed.

CHAPTER 12

By the time they reached the low-lying foot-hills Christie was ill with a chest cold and fever, suffering even more from the chill of the higher altitude. She now rode with her tattered blanket gathered about her slim shoulders, her bare feet feeling like lifeless chunks of cordwood.

The group as a whole was surly and snappish. The last of their meager food supply had been used that morning. The horses were slack-eyed and dispirited for want of grain and good feed.

The one bright spot for Christie was that their miserable circumstances had dulled Delwin's appetite for her. He had ceased running his eyes over her, had left off his touches, had apparently, at least for the time, lost interest in her altogether.

She hacked suddenly, then sneezed, discharging mucus from her nose. She turned at Delwin and grinned happily.

"Cold's gettin' better," she said brightly

and turned away, smiling.

Delwin growled something she could not quite make out.

"Goddamn, Pa," groaned Frankie. "My stomach thinks my throat's cut. We gotta git us somethin' to eat pretty soon."

"An' here you were thinkin' our baby brother didn't have no sense at all," Delwin, riding at Lance's side, muttered to his older brother.

"Goddamn sky don't have to fall on him, that's for sure," answered Lance. The two men grinned at each other.

"You boys be leavin' off pickin' on yer little brother," Deke Chambers joined in. "There be other ways of being gifted besides bein' smart. Just look at the way he dresses. He looks purtier than both of you dogs put together."

Frankie lapsed into sullen silence, and the ribbing eventually wore itself out.

"There's Brudsmore up ahead about ten mile," said Papa Deke. "We'll make out there, one way or other."

As he rode, Frankie contemplated a stain at the top of one of his doeskin moccasins, put there yesterday morning when he spilled his cup of coffee, the last of their coffee.

"I need some boots, Pa," he said. "If you're goin' to drag us up these mountains, I got to get somethin' warmer on my feet."

Papa Deke grunted his agreement. "But that little gal be needin' foot gear worsen you be. She gets down an' dies, she be no good for tradin' or nothin' else."

"I got me no use fer a dead wife, neither," said Delwin. He relished the quick, angry glance shot him by Christie.

They traveled a rocky trail angling up a gradual slope dotted with scrub pine and occasional patches of white-barked quaking aspen. Outcrops of dark red rock muted the splash of late mountain flowers. The air was sharp and clear, and sound seemed to carry forever.

As they climbed they heard the rattle of heavy wagons and harness, and steel-rimmed wheels on a rock road bed.

"Ore wagons," stated Papa Deke. A few minutes later they struck a wagon road and glimpsed the rear of an ore train pulling from sight beneath the heavy pines.

"Air's gettin' thinner, Pa," said Lance.

"We been climbin' steady. We got to remember to take it easy on the horses. They're weak anyhow. Ain't been gettin' enough to eat."

"I know the feeling," said Delwin. "When we get to town I be orderin' me a thick steak . . ."

"We ain't goin' to town — if I can help it," Deke said. "We got to be careful where we show our faces."

"How we goin' to get them supplies?" Delwin asked.

"An' my boots?" whined Frankie.

Deke gave his son a sour look, and Frankie immediately fell silent.

"We'll get whatever we need from folks what live on the outskirts. Later, when we get to Telluride, it be safe then to go into town."

He noted the silent disappointment on his sons' faces.

"We be all right, boys. We just got to think ahead of our pursuit. That's all."

"Pa," said Delwin, "nobody's after us. We ain't seen a sign for three, four days. My opinion he was got by them damn Utes."

"Could be," agreed his father. "Nevertheless, care be taken."

They continued north along the wagon road, occasionally encountering loaded ore wagons pulled by spans of mules.

At one point they were obliged to abandon the road while a train consisting of six wagons loaded with copper ore passed on the narrow road. Callous mule skinners, whips in hand, eyed them coldly as they passed.

When the last wagon rumbled by, spraying

them with fine red dust, Deke remarked, "They be givin' us a good oncet over." He looked at the girl, wrapped in her tattered blanket. "She be the cause. Sticks out like a sore thumb. We got to get her fixed out where she don't draw so much attention."

"Look there, Pa," exclaimed Frankie. He indicated a cabin a stone's throw from the road on the uphill side.

"Looks to be occupied," observed Lance.

They reined their horses off the road and approached the small cabin warily.

There was a squeal of laughter, and two small black children erupted from the open doorway. At the sight of the horsemen, the child in the lead, a tiny girl with tight, kinky braids, halted so abruptly the boy behind collided with her.

The children gazed upward at the horsemen with their wide, round eyes filled with sudden fear.

"Mama!" screamed the boy, spinning on his heels and racing for the cabin's porch. The little girl remained, transfixed.

A slim, attractive black woman appeared in the doorway, the boy clutching at her skirts. At the sight of the four disheveled and dirty men, her welcoming smile froze.

"What is it you want?" she asked, encircling the boy's shoulders protectively.

"How do, ma'am," said Deke Chambers with an open and friendly smile. His eyes darted about the small, neat cabin, the children, clean and brushed. His gaze lingered on the trim, groomed form of the woman.

"We be makin' a pilgrimage," he said, "my family an' me. We be headin' fer Denver an' we run onto hard times. We be buyin' a little food from you. If you can spare it."

The woman shook her head immediately. "No, sir, I cain't," she answered firmly. "We got just enough for our ownselves. Brudsmore's just a hoop 'n' holler down the road. You can git all you need there."

The little girl had retreated to the porch, to join her brother standing behind her mother's skirts.

Deke's smile deepened. He glanced about, indicating his sons and Christie.

"We be lookin' so ragged, ma'am, I was in hopes you might let us stop and clean up, rest a spell, an' maybe eat somethin' 'fore we move on into town."

The black woman shook her head again, adamantly. "My husband don't 'low us to entertain no strangers when he not around. Town will fix you up jus' fine." She turned to the door, shoving the children before her.

Delwin dropped suddenly from the saddle, bounded up the porch steps, and laid a rough, restraining hand on the woman's arm.

"Just hold on, ma'am," he said, grinning. "You got no call bein' rude."

She recoiled from his touch, trying in vain to break his iron grip.

"You turn me loose! Children!" she screamed. "Run! Out into the back woods!"

The children disappeared like little sprites, bolting from sight into the cabin.

"Lance! Frankie! Get around back an' snake 'em up!" Papa Deke dropped from the saddle. He ordered Christie, "Missy, don't you move!"

Christie's heart hammered against her ribs with a new, choking fear. She longed to drive her heels into the ribs of the paint mare and go thundering away down the rutted wagon road, but she knew they would follow after and run her down. And when they had her again, Papa Deke would likely allow Delwin to make good his threat to make the whispering wind to blow across her backside. Her escape attempt must wait. She must have better odds.

She sat on the paint, listening to the sounds of struggle from within the cabin. In too short a time it grew quiet, save for the sobs of the two frightened children. They had them, Christie languished. They had the children, and all was lost.

★ ★ ★

Christie huddled against the outside cabin wall beneath the porch overhang, holding the two children to her own thin, wasted frame. Their small black faces were pinched with terror as they watched their mother suspended from a porch rafter beam by ropes around her wrists. Only the tips of her toes could reach the plank floor, and her wrists were swollen from the tight ropes.

The crash of overturning furniture, the rattle of trashed dishes, pots, and pans came from inside. Of the men, Lance alone remained outside to keep an eye on the prisoners while the others searched the cabin.

The children clung to Christie, weeping silently, while she whispered little feeble bits of encouragement in their ears.

"I want Mama," wailed the girl, tears streaming down her cheeks.

Her mother managed to turn on the ropes to see her child. In agony, from the ropes and the strained position of her arms, she yet managed a brave smile.

"Hush, child," she said through clenched teeth. "We ain't done fer yet. We got us a secret these bad men don't know about. Daddy be home soon. Then you jus' head fer cover, honey, 'cause the fur's goin' to fly."

"Yeh, an' you'll find Daddy strung up there

right alongside you, too." Frankie sneered, striding about in a pair of black leather boots, acres too large for him. "One thing I can say — if your man fits these boots, he's one whole hell of a nigger."

Delwin stuck his face out the cabin door. He threw an armload of clothes at Christie. "Here, get into these," he ordered, and withdrew again into the cabin. The next item tossed out was a pair of button-top shoes, black leather, smallish, like the children's mother might wear.

"I said get into them clothes," Delwin exploded, observing the clothes lying at Christie's feet. "I be sick an' tired of hearin' you moan an' complain about bein' cold."

Christie obeyed numbly. She released herself from the children and began slipping the calico dress over her head, fighting her arms into the sleeves. The dress looked quite new, and she wore it over her pants and Navajo shirt.

"Ma'am," she whispered, fastening the buttons at the dress front, "I ain't with them. An' I'm sorry for you. I never stole nothin' before in my life."

The resilience had drained from the woman's spine. She hung now like a side of meat on a hook, eyes glazed, lips waxen.

"Ma'am, don't give up. Please," begged

Christie. "Don't give up."

The woman managed a weak smile. "Don't let them hurt my babies," she whispered.

Christie was frantic. She turned on Lance. "Make them stop this, damn you! You're not like them. You'd never be doin' this on yer own!"

Lance looked at her stonily and then turned away, staring off down across the mountainside.

"Can't you see!" Christie screamed at him. "They're goin' to kill a woman and two children! Do you want to live with that the rest of your life?" She clenched her small fists in helpless fury. "If you were half a man you'd stop this!"

Lance hesitated, his back to the girl, the now unconscious woman, the two terrified children. He fingered the sheath knife at his belt, his eyes filled with disgust. A fatal certainty welled up within them, a grim and deadly resolve.

He turned slowly, drawing the knife. Christie's first reaction was to turn and run. She had never been so frightened in her life. She had pushed him too far.

Lance hesitated only a moment. He brushed past Christie, frozen in her new footwear, moved swiftly to the hanging woman. He drew one arm about her middle, supporting her,

103

reached overhead and slashed the ropes holding her suspended.

She fell like a sack of sand.

With one grateful glance at Lance, Christie rushed to the woman and fumbled loose the ropes still clinging to her tortured wrists. The children, weeping, clung to the prostrate form of their mother.

"Don't be doin' this to your family, Lance." The voice of Papa Deke cracked like the lash of Delwin's whip.

"They be innocent folks, Pa," said Lance, and Christie noticed for the first time something in his voice other than grumbling anger. It was stark fear. "Let's just take what we need and leave. There's no cause to be hurtin' them."

"Defy me?" screamed Deke Chambers. "Defy me?"

The faces of Delwin and Frankie appeared in the open doorway, the arms of Delwin loaded with food items, an apple wedged in his teeth.

"I'm gettin' tired, Pa!" Lance suddenly shouted back. "Always killin' an' hurtin'. I ain't goin' to take part in it no more!" He still held the knife in his clenched right hand, and he used it now in a reckless gesture.

Papa Deke took an involuntary step backward, eyes held on the flashing blade.

"Don't you threaten me, boy," he said from behind a knot of fear. "I be yer pa."

Confused, Lance looked to the knife in his hand, slipped it absently back into its sheath.

"I weren't threatenin' you, Pa," he said sullenly. "But I meant what I said. I'm through with livin' this way."

The old man's eyes showed relief. Delwin and Frankie remained framed in the doorway, eager to see what was to happen next.

"Lance," Deke Chambers said gruffly, "you always done what I tell you — ever since you were a little boy. It ain't no different now. You know what we be after. These be worthless people an' —"

"They ain't worthless," Christie said. She rubbed at the deep welts on the woman's arms. "They're people. Human beings. Like Hap was." Tears began to spill down her dirty cheeks. "You're the devil!" she screamed at Deke.

In one step he was at her side. He raised his hand and brought it down across the side of her head, knocking her across the unconscious woman's prostrate body.

Christie lay in a crumpled heap, mockingly resplendent in her new dress, an utterly pathetic figure.

She made no move to get up, content with

covering her face with her arms and softly sobbing.

"You do that again," said Lance evenly, "an' I'm leavin'. An' I'm takin' the girl with me."

"Well now, dear brother," Delwin barbed, easing from the door and dropping his burden of loose food on the porch. "Me an' Pa an' Frankie might jus' have somethin' to say about that." As he moved, slowly circling, he slipped the ever-present bullwhip from over his shoulder. "I made up my mind. Since we got nobody to ransom the girl to, I be takin' her as my wife, just as soon as we get to Telluride." His voice was low and menacing.

"If you're lookin' to put fear into me, Delwin," Lance answered, just as savagely, "you're wastin' yer time. An' if you come at me with that whip, I'll guarantee you'll wind up eatin' it." Lance's hand moved to the butt of his six-gun. "And as fer marryin' Christie, I'll see you in hell first."

Frankie tittered happily from the doorway. "Oowee! We got us an all-out war, just on yer account, little girl. Ain't you ashamed, you little hussy?"

"There'll be no war between my sons," said Deke Chambers. "There ain't no woman worth killin' a brother over. Delwin, put that goddamn whip away. And you, Lance, you

106

back off! You hear me now? The both of you!"

Grudgingly Delwin slipped the coiled whip back over his shoulder.

Lance's fingers on his right hand flexed once more and then relaxed.

"Get up, gal," Lance said to Christie. "We be goin'. An' there ain't no one goin' to hurt this woman or her kids." And he looked defiantly, first at Delwin and then at Papa Deke.

CHAPTER 13

The sun felt good on Cooper's back. He sat on a comfortable patch of warm sand, amid a cluster of boulders, watching the two small, efficient dogs work the hundred or so sheep past the cabin. The small boy walked nonchalantly behind, swinging a stick like a sword at clumps of sage. When he came abreast of Cooper, the boy tossed the stick aside and continued on soberly, black eyes looking dead ahead. Cooper started to raise his hand in a wave, but let it drop back onto the sand. No reaching that little Indian, he thought.

He did not hear her approach so much as he sensed her presence. She stood over him, her face indistinguishable, silhouetted as it was against the sun. Kneeling at his side, she delivered into his hand a tin cup of coffee.

"Thank you very much," he said quietly. "You shouldn't have gone to the trouble."

She remained silent for a full minute, black eyes watching the sheep, stone lips unmoving.

He sipped at the coffee, at the same time

staring after the sheep, but watching her now and then from the corner of his eye.

She was dressed in pants, a man's workshirt, roughed-out boots. A red bandana was knotted about her slim, brown throat.

When she spoke her voice was a soft, sad monotone.

"I've felt bad," she said, "about the way I treated you."

"You've been very good to me," he answered, surprised. "Hadn't been for you I could be dead now. You saved my life."

She shook her head, directed her glittering black eyes upon his. "It was my fault your wound reopened. And it was my fault the men you were after got away."

He set the cup on the sand. "They haven't got away — not by a damn sight. They just got a little more time, that's all. Besides, I'm a grown man. It was my idea to get up too soon."

"I drove you to it," she insisted stubbornly.

He let it go. She was obviously intent on self-recrimination this morning.

He turned back to admire the freshness of the desert. It had rained the night before, and the air smelled washed and clean. The sky was clear but for a few lacy clouds, and the sun cast everything in a warm, lemon glow. A day of strength and life, but a dying day.

October was half-gone, and days like this were numbered.

There would be snow in the mountains now, slowing down the movement of the four men and the girl. But those same conditions would also hamper Cooper's pursuit.

The woman broke into his thoughts. "My name is Clara Crandall."

Cooper could not restrain a smile.

"A strange name for an Indian?" she asked, her face expressionless.

"It isn't that," he answered quickly. "I've been here now — what, a week? And we're just getting around to introducing ourselves. Ben Cooper, ma'am. I'm real pleased to meet you." He extended his huge hand.

She looked at it a moment, and then placed within it her own small hand. Her grip was firm and brief, and she quickly withdrew it.

"I take it Crandall was the boy's father?" he said. "What happened to him?"

"He was killed by white men, raiders from the south. They shot and killed most of our sheep. Ran off the rest. When he tried to stop them, they shot him." She spoke dispassionately. "Thad was three. We've survived on our own since then.

"I considered returning to my people. But I had to think of Thad. The Indian way is dead. He's half-white and he needs to be raised in a white man's world, with a white man's chances. I can at least give him a start here. I've taught him to read. I've been able to put some money aside from the sheep. When he is older, I'll send him to the white man's school."

As she talked Cooper's eyes roved about her fine features. She was still quite beautiful, but in the bright yellow sunlight he noted flaws he had not noticed before. Her sharp, aquiline nose had been broken midway down. It took a very slight turn to the left. There was a series of small white decorative scars running along her sharply defined chin on both sides.

Cooper finished his coffee. "Well, you've picked one hell of a hard road for yourself. Ain't many women would hang on like you have."

"I had no choice," she said simply. "Just as you have no choice."

He looked into her serene, unsmiling face. "No choice?"

"About the men. No matter what the risk to yourself, you must go after them. That commitment is what makes you the kind of man you are."

A chill breeze from the southwest had picked up and it tugged at the ends of her long black hair.

Cooper shivered. He felt suddenly very

tired, very weak. He had lost much weight, and the lines in his face, the weariness in his eyes, made him look suddenly and for a moment very old.

"You need to rest," she said, rising. "I'll help you back."

He got slowly to his feet. Though he had navigated on his own from the house to his little nest in the warm sand, he now leaned gratefully on her strong, young shoulder. Her arm clung supportingly about his waist.

She walked him slowly, unhurriedly back to the cabin, unaware of the black, smoldering eyes of her son upon them.

He had given her back her own bed several nights before, adamant against her protests, and had instead claimed a small, horsehide cot in the supply room off the kitchen lean-to.

He appeared ashen-faced and drawn as she slowly lowered him to the edge of the cot. With an effort he unbuckled his heavy gunbelt and placed it carefully on the floor beside him.

When she began to remove his boots, he made a half-hearted protest, which she ignored. She forced him gently back on the cot and covered him with a blanket.

"I'll wake you in an hour," she said. "Too much sleep in the day can spoil your night's rest." She placed a cool hand on his forehead. A fever still burned low, and again she felt a twinge of guilt. The infection he had been battling had been mostly the result of the wound reopening. And she could not forget the circumstances that had led to his getting up too soon.

Her hand lingered a moment longer than necessary, resting on his forehead in wistful human contact. His eyes closed slowly.

After a moment she withdrew. She pulled the heavy curtain halves together in the lean-to's doorway and turned, nearly colliding with her son.

He stood rock silent, obsidian eyes looking into hers, accusing.

"He is well enough to leave," the boy stated, his voice somewhat louder than usual.

She took him by his thin shoulders, turned him about, and marched him from the small kitchen into the cabin's front room. She turned him to face her and looked him sternly in the face. "He's still very weak, Thad."

"He's strong enough to ride. He can make it into town. Someone can help him there." He stood arrow-straight before his mother.

She could not help thinking how he had grown, over six inches in the past year. It was to be expected — his father, Crandall, had been a large man, over six feet. The boy showed a tendency toward height and lean-ness, a very definite non-Ute trait. Secretly she was pleased. A bigger man, even though half-Indian, would have it easier in the outside world. Men instinctively respected big men.

"Why do you dislike him?" she asked directly. "Has he said or done something to upset you?"

"He is white. And he is weak," the boy answered with an air of superiority.

"Have you forgotten your father was white?"

A muscle twitched in the boy's cheek. "He was also weak."

She looked intently at the boy for a moment, and then she stepped into the kitchen, poured herself a cup of coffee. Returning to the front room, she seated herself in her rocking chair, the one made for her by the boy's father. She motioned the boy to a seat on the couch.

"I've known for some time of the resentment you've had toward your father. It is time we deal with it."

The boy's eyes glowed strangely. He had always been a very respectful, obedient little boy, and now she wanted to be very careful she did not crush that little flower. She must not, her heart told her, come down on him too hard. She must listen respectfully to his feelings.

"Why do you think your father was weak, Thad?" she asked. She gave him time, sipping her coffee, looking at him patiently over the cup.

"A weak sheepherder," he answered grimly, "who couldn't even protect his sheep — or his family — or himself."

"He died trying to defend us. No man could have done more."

"A Ute would not have allowed himself to be preyed upon so," he answered defiantly. "Lame Badger says —"

"Lame Badger," she repeated softly. "When I saw your new moccasins, I guessed he had been to see you again. When was he here?"

"Yesterday. He is growing anxious. He wants us to return to our people. He wants to be my father. He wants to be your husband."

"I will choose my own husband, Thad, when the time comes," she said flatly. "I need no seven-year-old boy to make my choice. Lame Badger is a hothead who would stir up more trouble between white and Indian and end up making the Utes' condition worse than it already is."

"He is a brave man," insisted the boy angrily. "Even now he bears the marks of battle on his body. He rides tall. He needs no woman to nurse him."

With difficulty she reined her temper. He

had never spoken to her in this manner. Though she had never before tolerated insolence from her son, this issue was too important, too dangerously explosive. She could not risk alienating him. She would not drive him to Lame Badger.

"Lame Badger preys on the weak and the helpless. If he were a real man he would not try to turn a son against his mother."

The boy's eyes wavered and then fell. "I would never go against you, Mother," he insisted plaintively. "But you are wrong about Lame Badger."

She set her cup on the table and placed a tender hand on his shoulder. "We shall see. Go saddle the horses, Thad, while I leave a note for the marshal."

The boy looked up, wonder in his large black eyes.

"We will go and talk with this wonderful Lame Badger of yours," she said. "Perhaps he will have more luck swaying me in person than he has had by using my little boy against me."

CHAPTER 14

"I think I got 'im that time," Frankie whispered. A moment later a rifle bullet tore off a chunk of wood from the fallen log behind which he was hiding and flung it in his face. He fell over backward, howling. When he reappeared, his face was a mask of blood.

"You all right, boy?" asked Papa Deke.

"Hell no, I ain't all right!" Frankie wailed. "Can't you see all the blood. I'm hurt real bad!"

"Quit yer whinin'," said Delwin. "You just got whopped with a little piece of wood. Bullet didn't come nowhere near ya."

Frankie sat on his knees, rocking, red-smeared hands pressed to his face.

"Head wounds always bleed a lot," consoled Papa Deke. "Even little scratches."

They lay concealed among the rotting wooden corpses of a deadfall. When the shooting had started they had dived from their horses to the closest cover available. Now the firing had run off their mounts, and unless they quickly got whoever was doing the shooting they would all be left afoot. Even now, spooked as the horses were, they would have a hard time running them down.

Christie lay on her stomach, her cheek pressed against the dank, rotting leaves. The old coat the black woman had given her was pulled up to her ears and she tried to make herself small within it. She was scared. The bullets were flying too close to her, and she wished fervently she had taken a little more time to select her cover. The twisted pile of slim, dead branches scarcely concealed her. It would take nothing at all for a bullet to weave its way between them and find her out.

The men had each found excellent cover behind more dense sections of the deadfall. Frankie was the only casualty thus far, and the wound he suffered was more a result of his own folly than inadequate cover.

"Reason with him, Pa," said Delwin. "Tell him we be givin' the food an' stuff back. Maybe he let down his guard long enough we can drop him. Sure would be fine to take 'im alive though." He licked his lips at the prospect.

"Can't believe I raised such a fool," mumbled Deke Chambers. "Idiot. You actually think he gives a damn about what we took? He be after the man who strung up his wife.

Let's see, that be you, warn't it, Delwin?"

Delwin looked at his father. "I ain't scared of no nigger," he said without much conviction. "He gets too close he's liable to be feelin' a little draft on his backside."

Lance chuckled from his secure shelter. "From the one glimpse I got of that ol' boy, he be big enough to make you eat that damn whip. If I was you, Del, I think I be buryin' it."

Delwin looked angrily at his brother but said nothing. But he thought, if Lance didn't quit sending barbs his way all the time, he could easily see the day when that little old breeze be whistling up his own backside. Even as he mulled such thoughts he knew it could never happen. Pa wouldn't allow it, and unless he was somehow rendered helpless, Lance was far too formidable with guns, knives, and fists for Delwin to ever come out on top in a fair fight. Delwin preferred by far to use his whip on those helpless.

Delwin cast a glance at Christie. From his position he could see only her shoes, but that was enough. He needed only to reassure himself that she had not slipped away. He wasn't about to lose that gal. No, sir. He had come to think of the girl in most possessive terms. The idea of marriage had started as just another way to torment her. But as the idea took root in his mind Delwin found it more and more to his liking. She wasn't bad looking — clean her up a bit, get her out of those old jeans and into a pretty dress, ribbons in her hair and what not.

Thoughts of Christie in the role of a woman made Delwin think of the other women in his life — saloon girls mostly, professional women whose affection for him faded in direct proportion to his dwindling funds. In the course of a hundred encounters he became bitter and disillusioned, treating the women with contempt and sometimes outright cruelty. Furthermore, the endless string of roadside encounters left him feeling empty and frustrated, longing for something just a bit more wholesome and lasting, and of a far less commercial nature.

Not that he ever considered that a woman could actually love him or want to stay with him. But the right one, caught young enough and trained right, might learn to accept life with him as a matter of course.

Christie was young enough. And if the Chambers family could ever get together a strike large enough to establish some permanence to their existence, she just might come around to Delwin's bedside of her own volition. After all, he ruminated, life with Delwin Chambers could not differ so much from that she had shared with that old bastard Hinkle.

And that was another damn good reason for hanging onto the girl: Hinkle. Delwin was still not completely convinced that there was no money hidden. Hap Hinkle had been one of the most successful stage robbers in the history of the sport. Law enforcement officials and Wells Fargo agents had sighed with collective relief when he had hung up his guns and white hood and retired.

Out of all the money he had stolen he must have had something left. Him and the girl didn't live on daydreams. And it was a hell of a long shot to think he was prospecting enough out of that desert to support them.

Delwin's eyes squinted as he concentrated. For damn sure, if there had been any gold stashed away, the girl would know. She would have to know.

A bullet struck a rock a few feet from his head, spraying the side of his face with hot little fragments. He cursed and burrowed deeper behind his cover.

"You, girl!" he called to Christie. "Worm your way back here. You ain't got enough cover there."

The girl did not move, thinking that perhaps getting shot was more desirable than moving next to Delwin.

Another bullet clipped a branch in two just above her head.

"Take that hat off!" ordered Delwin. "Show him yer a girl."

Christie complied with that order, taking off the battered hat, holding it quickly aloft, and then lifting her head briefly to give the shooter a quick look at her long hair.

A great booming voice came from a matted thicket across the road.

"I sees ya, missy. You jus' lay still so's I knows where ya at. My woman say what ya did fo' her — you an' the quiet one. My fight ain't with you folks, an' you an' the man are free to leave if you can manage it. The rest of us folks," he continued with a voice of brittle metal, "why, we jus' goin' to set here awhile an' think 'bout all we did wrong."

"What you shootin' at us fer?" called Papa Deke, the black crown of his hat cresting the log behind which he lay.

A rifle bullet lifted the hat neatly from his nearly bald crown and tossed it twenty feet behind him, lost in a berry thicket.

"I'm shootin' at you — an' I'm a killin' you — 'cause a man oughts to be able to leave his family alone whilst he goes out an' earns them a livin'. I'm shootin' at you 'cause a decent woman don't be needin' strung up that-aways. An' I'm shootin' 'cause little babies need to feel safe in their own homes. I'm shootin' 'cause you're worse'n snakes and varmints an' somebody needs to put they foot on yer head an' squish!"

The heavy rifle boomed again, and a branch thick as a man's wrist, suspended above Delwin's head, dropped on the cowering form.

Delwin was unhurt, but he was scared. The black man had said the girl could go. And the quiet man with her. Now how did he know which one was the quiet one? It could just as easy be a fella by the name of Delwin as one with the name of Lance.

"Missy!" he hissed. "You, girl!" He eased forward a bit, full-length on the ground, extended his rifle muzzle, and touched the sole of Christie's shoes. "Christie, you holler an' tell him you want to leave, an' to hol' his fire." He glanced over his shoulder at Papa Deke, who lay some fifteen feet to his rear. He hoped the old man had not heard his whispered instructions to the girl.

Since Christie had been considering just such action — the first clear chance at escape offered to her — she made to comply.

"Tell him," hissed Delwin, "you be takin' the quiet one with you."

Christie raised her hand first, then her shoulders.

"I sees ya, missy." The big voice reverberated among the pines and rocks. "You go ahead and git now. If you a mind to, an' kin find yer way back, head for my house. My woman be glad to hep ya."

Christie rose hesitantly to her feet.

"Tell 'im, fer God's sake!" croaked Delwin.

Papa Deke started to rise, then recalled the fate of his hat. He settled instead for calling out to the rifleman. "The girl stays. She's family."

"No. She ain't family," answered the thunderous voice. "She don't slink and squirm along the ground likes the rest of you does."

Christie took a few faltering steps from behind the tangle of limbs.

"Christie, by damn!" Delwin abandoned the whisper. "Tell 'im I'm the quiet one!"

The girl looked over her shoulder and said, "Go to blazes." She skipped agilely across the tangled footing. When she reached the road she ran.

"You little double-crosser!" screamed Delwin. He planted the bead on his rifle sight in the middle of the girl's back.

Just as his finger tightened on the trigger, Lance, unmindful of the threat from the thicket, raised himself up. He pointed his rifle at Delwin.

"Delwin, you shoot that girl an' I swear I'll kill you!"

At that moment the hidden rifle boomed. The bullet took Lance in the neck, cleanly severing his spine. He dropped without a sound, and his rifle discharged harmlessly into the trees above the road.

For a moment there was silence, broken only by the sound of Christie's running shoes on the rocky roadbed.

CHAPTER 15

The village was a cluster of tattered skin-covered huts, maybe twenty in number, pitched without any recognizable plan or order in the bottom of a small, dry basin.

The woman and the boy had ridden northeast for two hours, unerringly following the ill wind blowing from the camp.

"So you think you want to live like this?" she asked the boy as they walked their horses between the huts. Scrawny, scavenging dogs skulked along behind them. Ragged children sat playing in the dust. "Do you think living here will make you grow up to be a warrior? Do you really believe that, Thad?"

Again the strange light in the boy's eyes. "This is now," he said between clenched teeth. "It will not always be this way. Lame Badger will tell you."

She slapped her horse with the reins, biting her lip to keep from an angry reply.

At the largest of the lodges they dismounted. She stepped up to the closed flap and called,

"Little Owl, it is the daughter of Coyote. I would speak with you."

A voice, cracked and feathery as the parchment cover of the hut, called out, "The daughter of my old friend dead these many winters is welcome."

She lifted the flap and, with the boy in tow, stepped into the smoky interior.

They had to step carefully. The small, smoking fire was surrounded by reclining blanketed forms, some full-length, some with arms or legs overlapping their neighbor.

Little Owl and one shrouded figure in the corner were the only two upright forms.

"Sit, daughter," he invited, indicating an open spot to his left.

She knelt. A man would have sat cross-legged, but custom bade the woman kneel. She put the boy down firmly beside her.

She needed no explanation for the sleeping forms about her. These dejected and beaten Indians had managed to escape the white man's world in the only way left to them.

In front of Little Owl, on a flat rock, were arranged the buttons of the peyote, the small green disc that when chewed, transported the aged chief and his old warriors back to the days of their glory, when they rode the mountains and the western slope free, when they hunted what they needed, when they needed for nothing beyond that which they could provide themselves.

Little Owl's rheumy eyes gazed at the young woman. He exposed shrunken, naked gums in a loose smile.

"The daughter of my old friend fares well," he said in his coarse whisper. "The boy grows strong and tall, like Crandall."

She nodded. "He is like his father in many ways."

The old chief held up one withered hand. He took the woman's hand in his, dropped into her palm one of the small green buttons.

With her thumbnail she scraped at it, carefully removing the whitish outer covering, which could kill. When clean, she placed it in her mouth, chewed it to a green pulpy mass, and swallowed it.

"He is like his white father," she repeated. "But he is also like the Ute. He thinks the old ways are best."

They were silent for a time. The woman stared into the smoldering fire and watched, fascinated, as the flames grew larger and longer, turned a myriad of colors — long tongues, red, blue, green, yellow, licking, darting. She smiled dreamily and felt warm and relaxed.

"Yes," said the old man, "the old ways are best. But they are no more — only in the minds of old men, and in the cactus."

The hut flap was jerked open, sending harsh light knifing into the eyes of those within.

A tall form stooped down, then stepped into the murky interior. Thad started to rise, but the woman pulled him down sharply.

She looked up through the yellowed, smoky light into a handsome, bronzed face with features much like her own, sharply defined and clean, with none of the squashed contours of the Ute. He was broad and well muscled. His black eyes pierced into her own, and a pleased light glowed in their depths.

"I did not expect you to come so soon," he said, breeching protocol and ignoring the chief. "But I am pleased you came."

"I did not come to stay," she answered flatly. "I came because you have been upsetting my son, driving a wedge between him and me. I came to ask you to leave us in peace."

The eyes hardened. He shook his head and glanced about at the blanketed, hallucinating bodies. He reached suddenly across the fire with one powerful arm, grasped her wrist, and pulled her to her feet.

"This is no place to speak of these matters. This is a house of the dead. We are the living."

She followed him from the hut, unable to resist his iron grasp on her arm. The boy followed eagerly, leaving the old chief to smile and nod into the flames.

Outside he released her and they squared off, as though to do battle.

"Go wait by the horses, Thad," she instructed.

The boy cast alarmed eyes at Lame Badger.

"Obey your mother," he ordered, his eyes never leaving hers.

"Don't take him too lightly," he said to her when the boy had moved reluctantly away. "If one wants to raise a son to be a good warrior, one must treat him with respect at an early age."

"I do not need your advice on raising my son," she answered evenly. "I want him to be raised as a white man."

"He is Ute," Lame Badger said simply.

"The Utes are dead." She pointed at one of the scrawny, slinking dogs. "There," she said derisively, "are the Utes. They sneak from here to there, stealing what they can, stealing from each other."

Lame Badger's chin lifted, his shoulders squared. She noticed a deep, scabbed-over furrow across one shoulder.

"Had you listened to your son you would know. These" — he swept a scornful gaze around the ragged camp — "are dead men's bones. I lead the warriors. I draw to me all the young men and their young wives. I tell them all to have many babies, for we are building a nation. These ones are old. They do not wish to fight to keep what is theirs. Their world is in the peyote. I will take you to our camp and show you. We eat good. We dress warm."

"No!" she answered, and fire danced in her eyes. "We are of the white man's world now. You take all your warriors and all your young men against the white man, and you will all die!"

He seemed not to have heard. "I will take you and the boy. I will be his new father. When he grows he will be my second in command. You will be my woman. You are still young. We can have many babies."

She laughed scornfully. "Don't be ridiculous. I would rather die than be your woman."

He smiled, unaffected. "Even so, if you continue to live, one day you will be my woman."

"You are the one who should worry about living. Maybe your life isn't so charmed after all." She pointed to the wound on his shoulder.

"It is a good omen," he proclaimed solemnly. "The span of one hand lower and I would be dead. I was protected." A look heavy with evil intent flared in his eyes. He smiled again. "Tell your friend, the lawman, I will come for him soon."

She gave one shocked look at the boy, standing sullenly with the horses.

"No," said Lame Badger following her gaze. "He did not tell me of the white man. Other eyes watch for me."

He pulled a long, wicked-looking knife from his belt. "Tell your white man I will eat his liver from the end of my knife. He killed four good warriors."

"You leave out the fact that you attacked him. The men he killed were trying to kill him."

"It does not matter," answered Lame Badger simply. "He must die. He is a brave man — he will die quickly. But he must die."

She was silent. There was no bargain to be made. She would not plead. A show of weakness would be the worst thing she could do.

One thing was certain, she had to get herself and the boy free of the camp. Cooper had to at least be warned.

Lame Badger's eyes gleamed with perception. "You care for this white man, daughter of Coyote. You think he will replace Crandall."

Her eyes wavered. "I need no one. I care for no one. The boy and I manage alone."

He ignored her denial. "You would save his life if you could." He slid the knife back under his belt. "Bargains have been made for much

less than the life of one wounded white man."
He paused a moment for her to consider. "You
agree to be my woman and he goes unharmed,
to pursue the four men and the young girl."

"You know even about them?"

He shrugged in a show of modesty. "No
one enters or leaves this land without my
knowledge. Those he seeks are trash. They
dress poorly. Their horses are poor. Even the
girl is thin and unattractive."

"And so you didn't want to waste your time
killing them," she finished for him.

He shrugged again. "They are of no importance to me. What is your answer?"

"I need time to consider," she countered.
"I will take the boy and go."

He smiled. "You need no time," he sneered.
"You have already decided. You wish only
to warn him." He motioned to the horses.
"Go. You are free, for now. I would not hold
you against your will. There may be a day
for that, but not today."

She left him standing, arms folded across
his muscled chest, confident smile on his lips.
She hurried to her waiting son. The boy
started to speak, but she shot him a stern
warning glance.

"Get mounted," she said.

CHAPTER 16

Cooper lay on the narrow cot in his tiny room. He listened to the rain, driven by the wind, peck at the window above his head. From beyond the blanketed doorway came the sounds of the woman stirring about the kitchen. It was late afternoon and the light was waning, too dim to continue with his reading. His eyes were weary anyway.

He raised up and looked through the window at the desolate landscape. It even looked cold now, in a way more savage and uninviting than when in the scorching grip of the summer months.

If it was raining down on the flatlands it would mean snow in the mountains.

He found himself thinking of the young girl, and again the restlessness to be on his way took hold. The woman said the wound was improving, yet weakness plagued his every effort.

That morning, before the rain had begun, he had tried to take another walk but had returned to the house, light-headed and sweating, after covering only a few hundred feet.

When he collapsed in the rocking chair the woman had looked at him sternly, saying nothing. He knew he was pushing it. He had been gravely wounded, and he needed more time to recover fully. That, he realized grimly, was not possible. If he were ever to do the girl any good, it must be soon. Each day gave the four killers opportunity for digging in and disappearing in the mining towns and backwoods settlements of the San Juans.

The woman had changed. Since she and the boy had returned the previous afternoon she was restless and pensive, almost angry, snapping at the boy and giving only terse reply to Cooper's attempts at conversation. Something had happened during the course of their ride, but there was little chance, Cooper conceded sadly, of extracting anything from an Indian until he — in this case, she — was ready to tell it.

He raised the blanket and entered the kitchen, walking past the silent woman, stopping just long enough to pour himself a cup of coffee from the pot on the back of the wood range.

In the front room he eased himself into the hardback rocker parked before the fireplace. Settling back, he sipped at the coffee and let himself be hypnotized by the dancing flames.

Presently she entered the room, cup in hand, and drew up a chair facing him. It was now time to talk, he gathered.

"Where's the boy?" he inquired.

"He's out in the shed, grooming your horse, I think. He's taken a liking to the animal." She looked at him with her sad, black eyes glittering in the firelight. "We have only the two old dray horses to ride."

Cooper nodded and smiled. "A great warrior needs a great horse to ride."

She did not answer his smile. "He must live in the white man's world. Soon 'Great Warrior' will be a term used to describe a lot of dead Indians. I want more for my son than to have him die with honor."

Cooper did not reply. He agreed that for the Utes it was a no-win situation. But did she realize, he wondered, how hard it would be for an Indian to amount to anything in a world overseen by a generation of whites convinced already of the inferiority of the red man? He felt sorry for her and her future disillusionment. It was pointless, he knew, for him to express his doubts. People need hope for the future just to survive the now.

"You must go," she said suddenly.

Although taken aback at her abrupt change of heart, he sipped his coffee calmly. "I'll leave first thing in the morning," he answered softly.

"No. It must be tonight. Now. As soon as possible."

He looked at her closely. She looked suddenly vulnerable, stricken. She had set the coffee cup to one side and her hands trembled.

"You're in great danger," she said. "The Utes you fought — who wounded you — Lame Badger is their war chief. He was there when you killed four of his warriors. He knows you are here."

His eyes narrowed, and she hastened to explain. "No. We did not tell him. Somehow he knew already. He is coming to kill you."

Cooper stared into his cup a moment. "Seems to me he tried that once already," he murmured.

She shook her head and looked at him with large worried eyes.

"Don't be a fool. How many warriors do you think you can kill in your present condition?"

He was silent for a time, then said suddenly, "Well, if that's the way it's to be, I'll not be bringing any more of my troubles upon you and the boy." He rose to his feet. "Wonder if you could have the boy saddle the horse for me while I get my stuff together?"

She nodded, rising. "Where will you go?"

She moved near him, dark lines of worry showing beneath the black eyes.

"Tell your friend Lame Badger if he wants me, I'll be headed east, to the mountains."

"You're still going after the girl? You'll never make it."

The tarp containing his blanket roll was tied behind his saddle. He stood in the doorway, hat in hand, the rain slicker she had given him draped over his wide shoulders. Behind him the rain drove down in a slanting wall, obscuring everything beyond a hundred yards distance.

"Thank you, Clara," he said simply. "Without you I would have died. If I could repay you, I would. Chances are we'll never see each other again."

She nodded. She was surprised at how vulnerable he suddenly looked to her, his shoulders hunched forward, shirt and pants hanging loose on his frame.

"I am ashamed to drive you out now, only half-well. You should return immediately to Mexican Hat. You will not find them anyway — those you follow. Too much time has passed. You're too weak."

He grinned lamely. "Don't count me out yet. I'll toughen up once I hit the saddle."

The boy stood in the rain, silent, holding

the steeldust's reins and speaking to the animal in low tones.

She came to him then, reaching her mouth up to his, her arms circled about his neck. His long arms pulled her slim body to his, and they stood thus for a time, expressing in the embrace everything for which they had no words.

When she released him, extricating herself from his grasp, he turned and stumbled through the door into the rain.

The boy stared up at him, eyes wide and full of resentment.

"Take care of your mother, boy," Cooper said, taking the reins from the small brown, reluctant hands. "Remember, son, a man has to think of those who are depending on him before he can think of himself."

The boy went to his mother and they stood in the open doorway, watching Cooper ride away in the driving rain.

CHAPTER 17

The snow enveloped her in a cold, white blanket, snuffing out her view of the path ahead, muffling the sound of her pursuers.

Christie stopped for a moment, resting in the shelter of a rock bank, and examined the footprints she had left in the snow. If she could only get far enough ahead, the snow would fill in her tracks and she would be safe. But safe for what? To freeze? To starve?

She shivered and started on, pulling the coat closer about her. Her feet, feeling like frozen stumps, seemed to have a will of their own, wandering from the easier going of the game trail off into the thickets of snow-covered laurel.

Her toe struck a rock and she fell, thrusting her bare hands beneath the snow. Her palms were slashed on the sharp stones, and she knelt in the reddening snow and cried, deep ragged sobs.

That is how they found her, Papa Deke, Delwin, and Frankie. So deep was her anguish and frustration they stood their horses behind her for several moments before she became aware of them.

Finally she looked up with sodden, miserable eyes, the picture of suffering. Her spirit was broken. Somewhere in the back of her mind, she welcomed them. They, at least, had provided fire and some occasional bits of food. Now, without them, she would die.

Five hours before she had struck out, as the voice from the thicket had advised her, to return to the cabin. The black woman would care for her, she would be warm, and when the woman's husband returned they would all be safe. But she had lost her way when the rain began. And when it turned to snow she panicked, running without direction until she was exhausted, scratched, and bleeding.

Delwin dropped from the saddle and picked her up from out of the snow. He led her to her little paint horse, wrapped a blanket about her quaking frame, and lifted her into the saddle. The four set off wordlessly down the trail.

An hour's ride brought them to a small box canyon, free of the wind at least, and with several deadfalls for dry firewood.

Christie was allotted the job of gathering wood for a fire while the three men threw together a makeshift shelter of pine branches and boughs. When finished it was roomy and tight enough so they could spread their beds out of the snow.

It was a cold, silent camp. They ate a meal of canned beans and pork, hardtack and coffee, all taken from the black family's cabin.

When the pain in her stomach had been satisfied, and her tortured hands warmed by the flames, Christie set about stockpiling wood to see them through the night.

The men were ragged, on edge. They had survived an ordeal and they needed a rest. While their condition was not nearly as desperate as her own, Christie wondered at their vacant, hollow-eyed appearance. Even Frankie was subdued, clothes ragged and soiled, hair disheveled, lips parted in a breathless, panting attitude.

She spread her one blanket in a far corner of the lean-to and crawled between its folds. Papa Deke, Delwin, and Frankie remained silhouetted against the flickering flames, drinking coffee and talking in muffled tones.

By lying still and pretending to sleep she was able to overhear most of what was said, piecing together what had happened after she made her escape.

Lance was dead, killed by the husband of the woman they had terrorized. The gun of the black man had been silenced by rifles from a passing ore wagon. The two men on the wagon had believed the story Papa Chambers had hastily concocted and, as a courtesy, had gone after their horses and found all five animals.

They buried Lance after the ore wagon moved on, scooping out with their tin plates a shallow trench for his body, piling rocks and leaves over the mound. And then they went after the black man.

In the thicket from which he had fired upon them they found only empty cartridge cases and a few smudged bootprints, quickly obliterated by the freezing rain.

They had more luck following after Christie, who was their primary concern anyway. The girl's fatal mistake lay in following the two-rutted wagon road too long. When she finally stepped from the road, it had begun to snow, and her footprints, though rapidly filling, could be followed easily by someone close behind on horseback.

CHAPTER 18

Ben Cooper bore her no resentment. Had he stayed, the Utes would sooner or later put in an appearance. In the ensuing fight — he could never give himself up to them — the woman and her son would be endangered, retribution, perhaps, made against them for harboring the white man. Since they had saved his life, he owed them better than that.

His mind dwelt on the woman's abrupt and surprising embrace. He had tasted passion on her lips — passion born of loneliness, days of solitary toil and responsibility, the need of a woman to be held and cared for. And for just that one moment he had tried to answer that need, responding out of instinct, without thought to the consequences.

Would he ride back this way after rescuing the girl? Cooper did not want to think about the answer to that. Jane Porter waited for him in Mexican Hat. And while they had no formal agreement between them, he knew the lady and he shared a tacit understanding. That, in his mind, was as good as a solid commitment.

He smiled grimly. Here he was, riding along in the rain, barely strong enough to hold himself up in the saddle, Indians perhaps on his trail at the very moment, and he was trying to sort out his problems with women. The one little female he should have on his mind, he reminded himself sternly, was the girl held captive by the four.

He rode steadily east, hoping to put several miles between himself and the cabin before dark. He counted on the rain to throw the Indians off should they attempt to overtake him. In his present weakened condition he could not afford a skirmish with Lame Badger. Even should he survive another fight, it would further jeopardize the girl's chances.

As he rode he cursed the circumstances that for so long had held him from following the killers. Cooper believed in the indifference of the law toward those it punished — revenge was not part of the picture. The law and its instruments of justice — peace officers, the courts, and the hangman — must be uninvolved emotionally. Cooper had fulfilled his duties for years on that basis. Now, on the trail of these cold-blooded killers who found pleasure in the torture of their helpless victims, Cooper imagined himself adjusting the rope around their necks with a sense of deep satisfaction. Whatever happened to the girl, the four would pay, full measure, pressed down and overflowing.

God help me, Cooper thought. God help me.

He awoke to a cloudless dawn and checked, first thing, his back trail. For miles toward the west he saw nothing but open, empty landscape, the sandy soil already looking dry and parched as though it had rained in the last century instead of last night. The vegetation — mesquite groves, prickly cactus, some sage — looked renewed and refreshed. All else bore the tired, enduring face of the desert.

He had rigged a makeshift tent, stretching his tarp across mesquite branches, and thrown his bedroll beneath. Even the short ride the night before had left him exhausted enough to fall immediately asleep, leaving the steeldust to warn him of approaching trouble.

Clara had stuffed his saddlebags with food. He rummaged out a small skillet, a small can for boiling coffee, some side meat, and a loaf of fresh-baked bread. He checked over his total stock of provisions and determined that if he were careful, he should have enough to see him through several days.

After his meager breakfast, he saddled the steeldust and then set about with a sage branch to brush out signs of the camp's existence. He knew it was likely a waste of time. No one tracked like Indians, and no Indians tracked better than the Utes.

He rode slowly throughout the day, resting often, at times walking and leading the horse. He needed to build his strength up as quickly as possible, because the rigors of the high country in winter — and he was sure that is where the pursuit would lead him — were severe enough to sap the vitality of even a strong, healthy man. Though he felt his wound was well along toward healing, he lacked the energy and the oxlike strength he had taken for granted all his life.

Two days later he approached the foothills of the San Juans rising above him to the east and north, blued by distance, dusted with snow, building to tall ragged peaks, white and forbidding.

It was hard to believe in the midst of all that cold and whiteness towns existed, mining communities thrived. The promise of gold and silver lured men to endure any privation, any suffering.

Cooper would need one of these towns soon. The steeldust needed reshoeing. For himself he would be needing a warm coat, supplies, a packhorse. And he would need information. At the moment he was riding blind. He hadn't the slightest indication of the direction his quarry had taken, only that their tracks had been pointing east when last he saw them. For now he must trust to his instinct. Eventually they would show, or some trace of them. They too would need supplies, and they would have to deal with people to get them, either stealing or buying.

He camped that night in a grove of aspen, leaves a flaming yellow, and threw his bedroll upon a mat of dried leaves he found in a tangle of fallen logs. The shrill bugling of elk nudged him awake in the crisp, gray dawn. During the winter, when snows covered their forage, the herds liked to dine on the tender white bark of the aspen. Cooper had noticed ample evidence of their presence the evening before. Their ear-rattling call bounced from rock to hillside and back, echoing, redoubling, until it sounded as though he were surrounded by a thousand of the beasts.

His camp lay on a gentle slope in the cleavage between two bare ridges. What little smoke arose from his cooking fire was scattered and dissipated by the branches of the aspen.

After eating he sat on a stump, drinking coffee, gazing down toward the wasteland below. There had been no pursuit by the Indians, and Cooper could not help but think that the woman had somehow taken care of that problem for him. He hoped the price she must have paid had not been too high.

CHAPTER 19

The boy sat at the table, picking listlessly at his plate. He had been so sure he would rejoice when the marshal rode out of their lives. He had been surprised and a little afraid at the strange, sad tug at his heart when the marshal disappeared beyond the driving rain.

It had angered him to see his mother kiss the man. It had filled him with resentment to see the man wear his dead father's clothes. But apart from these irritations, he found he missed the deep soft voice, the easy manner, and the warm smile. The marshal had shown only kindness to his mother, and gratitude for her help. He had never threatened, as had Lame Badger. Unlike the Indians, Cooper had treated his mother with respect.

"Eat your dinner, Thad," the woman said softly. "Your food is getting cold." She smiled lovingly at his small, sad face. "Are you sick?"

He shook his head and his black eyes once more found his plate.

She reached across the table and clutched

his little brown fingers. "It is not unmanly to share one's troubles with one's mother. Many times the Ute will ask advice from a woman — wife or mother — and though he will never admit it to another man, he listens to her counsel." She gave his fingers a squeeze. "And quite often it helps," she added gently.

He looked up slowly, his eyes shining.

"I thought I remembered my father — a little bit," he said thoughtfully. "But now the picture I had in my mind of him is muddy, like someone stepped in the water. Was he like the big white man?"

She searched his innocent, troubled face. "In many ways — I guess. They were both leaders of men. Both gentle and kind. Why do you ask, Thad?"

"You like the white man and you do not like Lame Badger. Lame Badger is a warrior, greater than the marshal. I don't understand. I saw you kiss the marshal, but you don't even speak kindly to Lame Badger. I thought it was because the marshal was like my father."

"Your father was a great man and a good man, Thad. He was also a foolish man to die for a bunch of sheep. But I loved him. I would never look for someone to take his place."

"Do you care for the marshal? You kissed him," the boy reminded.

She smiled a bit wistfully. "I care for him.

I don't think I realized it until he was about to leave."

The boy was silent. He looked distantly at the rain lashing the window and thought of the wounded white man riding alone through the wet and cold. "Why did the marshal run from Lame Badger? Doesn't a brave man always stay and face his enemies?"

"He left because I told him he must go. And he did not wish to endanger us."

Thad got up from his place at the table. "I will see to the horses," he said, slipping into his coat.

He had his hand on the door when she called to him. "You're old enough to work out such matters yourself. Remember, Thad, life is made up of judgments. How a boy sees things and people often tells what kind of man he himself will be."

Thad closed the door softly and stepped from the porch into the rain.

She had no indication of their presence until she opened her eyes and found the figure of Lame Badger towering over her bed.

With a cry she drew the bedclothes close about her.

"What are you doing in my house?" she demanded when she found her voice. "You sneak in like a thief to rob a helpless woman and her son." She bit off the words with contempt.

His answer came swiftly. He struck her in the face with his balled fist, driving her head back into the pillow, sending bolts of colored light shooting into her brain.

He reached down, grasped her shoulder roughly, and struck her again, this time with his open palm, and again with the back of his hand. She felt consciousness slipping and fought to turn away from the blows. Just when the blackness threatened to flow over her, he stopped.

He stood up from the bed, his chest rising and falling beneath his wet buckskin shirt.

"Your first lesson," he muttered, adjusting his belt laden with a revolver and a long knife. To her ringing ears his voice sounded far away. "You have the makings of a good squaw. Perhaps a few more beatings is all it will take."

Her lips were bleeding, but she managed to utter, "You had better kill me now. I will never be your squaw."

"The lawman has gone," he said scornfully. "He left you. He used you and left you — and now I claim you. You will return to your people, and you and the boy will live with me."

She lay motionless, her blood soaking the

pillow. Her black eyes glittered with hatred. "The lawman did not use me. I sent him away because he was wounded and could not fight. But he will return — and he will kill you like the dog you are."

He raised his hand to her again, and she shrank back into the bed. After a moment, he lowered the hand, the muscles of his jaws standing out in sharp relief.

"If he comes," he said tightly, "I will be waiting. And you will be waiting at my side."

"Never." It was a whispered denial, but it carried the weight of such conviction that the Indian blinked. "Leave my house," she ordered, "or kill me. If you do neither I will find a way to kill myself."

"You would leave the boy alone?"

"The boy will survive," she answered proudly. "Already he is more of a man than you will ever be."

He struck her again, viciously. Jerking his knife from his belt he raised it above his head, but suddenly he realized he was doing what she wanted.

His brown, handsome face broke into a smile, an evil, deadly smile. He replaced the knife in his belt.

Through the open bedroom door behind Lame Badger she saw the boy standing wide-eyed in the middle of the front room, while about him moved the dark forms of Lame Badger's warriors. From the living room came the sounds of destruction, wood splintering, glass breaking.

"I will not kill you, daughter of Coyote. Out of respect for your father who was once a great chief, I will let you continue to live as a white woman, if that is what you want. But your son is a Ute. He will come with me. I will raise him to be my son."

"No!" She started to rise from the bed, the covers falling away, exposing her thin gown. "You won't do this!"

"The Utes have many little boys. He will fit in well. We will raise them all to be warriors."

"Lame Badger, I swear if you take my son I will see you dead!"

"The choice is yours," he answered casually. "I take your son, burn your house, and you go live with the white man. Or you and the boy come with me." He smiled triumphantly, grabbed her arm, and jerked her from the bed. "Choose."

The light sleeping gown did little to conceal her well-rounded form, and he eyed her hungrily.

She snatched a blanket from the bed and quickly wrapped it about her. As she did so her eyes fell upon her son. The boy stood as though nailed to the floor. His eyes looked unbelievingly at the destruction happening about him. The Indians smashed and destroyed everything they did not want. Laughing and talking excitedly, they carried armloads of silverware, trinkets, blankets, and such out the door to their horses. Framed pictures, cushions, things he had seen about him all his young life were tossed about, smashed upon the floor, or torn apart by savage hands.

Through the open bedroom door their eyes met and held, the boy's eyes reflecting mute terror, her own trying to impart some message of comfort to her stricken son.

At last she turned to Lame Badger.

"All right," she answered softly, not looking upon his face — she could not bear to see him smirk. "I'll go with you."

His manner changed instantly. His smile was almost kindly.

"You will be happy," he said. "I will treat you well. I have another woman, and she will do things for you. You will be first."

She looked at him closely, holding the blanket fast about her. Hunger for her was in his eyes. It was true — he probably would treat her well. But at the first opportunity she and the boy would escape. She would bide her time. Her chance would come.

For a brief instant she thought of Cooper,

but just as quickly pushed the big white man from her mind. She could not rely on him. Should he survive encounter with the four men who had taken the girl, he would have been through quite enough. Even should he learn of her situation, she could not expect him to ride into an armed Indian camp to rescue an Indian woman and her son. Perhaps he agreed with Lame Badger; she and the boy were Ute, therefore they belonged with the Ute.

Lame Badger placed a hand on her shoulder. "I will be good to you," he promised. "You will learn to care for me."

"I am your prisoner," she said derisively. "Nothing more. And I will always hate you."

His smile faded, and a cold light glittered in his eyes. "You may hate me, but you will respect me, and you will be my woman." He pushed her roughly onto the bed and stalked to the door. "Get dressed. Gather clothes for you and the boy. We leave here!"

The rain had stopped and dawn was breaking when they rode out. She looked back at the empty cabin. White curtains billowed through the broken windows, destroyed household goods littered the front steps. Her throat constricted and she clutched the boy to her. They rode double on a small Ute pony. Behind, in the small stable, the dray horses lay dead, their throats slashed.

CHAPTER 20

Christie lay awake shivering, listening to the conversation of the three men by the fire. Occasionally their voices dropped to whispers — when they talked about her — and she strained to hear what was being said. With the death of Lance her predicament had sharply worsened; her only sympathizer was gone, and she was now totally at their mercy.

The men had been oddly silent in the days since the attack on the lonely mountain road. For a time Frankie had urged that they return to the black man's cabin and pay retribution for the killing of Lance. Papa Deke had other thoughts. He was himself suffering from the cold and wet, and he told them he longed for the comforts of a town, whiskey, and a woman — a real woman.

He had reached a decision concerning Christie, but for fear of Delwin's reaction, had thus far kept it to himself. He knew a man in Telluride who would pay several hundred dollars for the girl. Cleaned up, dressed right, she would earn her purchase price back in a few short weeks. The money for the girl would be enough to realize the Chambers family a fresh start. Not wealth, by any stretch of the imagination, but a start.

Papa Deke knew Delwin still had his mind set on getting the girl for himself. But Delwin must be made to see things in the light of what was best for the family. Delwin occasionally needed bringing in line. He had allowed how Lance's death had been caused by the girl, by her making a run for it. Papa Deke had had to restrain him at pistol point when, after they recaptured Christie, Delwin wanted to introduce her backside to his lash. The man in Telluride would pay little for damaged goods.

Christie lay now beneath her flimsy blanket, awaiting the dawn when they would strike out again. About the man in Telluride and Papa Deke's plans for her she knew nothing. When she had overheard him tell his sons they were going to Telluride, her heart had leapt, for where there were people, there was a chance for help and for freedom.

She did not know exactly how far Telluride was, but Papa Deke had said they would have to ride fast in order to beat the next storm. It was too cold to sleep. The men entered the lean-to, building the fire to a roar before rolling in their blankets. They lay staring at the flames until dawn.

Their breakfast was light. They were again low on food. But there was plenty of strong, hot coffee, and Christie gulped as much as they would allow her. Christie felt she needed to be alert, today above all, for she planned once again to try an escape. She was still quite run-down. The food they had stolen from the black family had not amounted to enough to do much good for a lot as impoverished as theirs.

As she mounted she looked doubtfully at the paint mare, now a mere shadow of the horse it had been when they started out. Could the mare carry her far enough and fast enough to put her beyond reach of the three men? A glance at their horses comforted her some. Their animals were in worse shape than the mare, and they were bound to carry a heavier load.

As they moved out Christie shivered. She had a sudden evil premonition about Telluride. . . .

Cooper walked the steeldust up to the cabin and dismounted. A thin column of smoke rose from the tin chimney, and the place had the look and feel of relaxed warmth.

"Hello the cabin," he called, stamping his

feet in the snow and working his arms for warmth.

A curtain at one of the front windows was lifted at each side, and two small black faces appeared. A moment later a tall, heavy black man in shirtsleeves stepped out on the porch. He held a shotgun in one hand, like a pistol.

"State your business, mister," he rumbled in a heavy bass voice.

"My name's Cooper. United States Marshal." He carefully pulled the flap of his coat aside, exposing his badge. "I'm looking for four men and a girl. Fella down at the Blue Bird Mine said you had a run-in with them."

The black man eyed him warily, and Cooper was glad he had announced himself and not come upon the man unawares. There was a dangerous glint in the dark eyes.

The two men stood a moment in silence, sizing each other up. At last the muzzle of the shotgun drifted to one side.

"Come in, Marshal. Coffee's hot." He turned and entered the cabin, leaving the door ajar.

After tying off the steeldust, Cooper mounted the wooden steps. He had to remove his hat and stoop to clear the doorway. When he straightened up it was to a room warm and clean and cozy.

It was a two-room cabin with beds in one

room in back, kitchen and sitting room in front. The cabin itself was not particularly well made, but it had been maintained well, indicating the family had, more likely than not, moved into it when abandoned and made it into a home.

The woman and two children stood before the stove, the children wide-eyed and curious, the woman smiling uncertainly.

"Seat yourself, Marshal," said the man, indicating a chair at the table. "This be my wife, Elizabeth, an' them two imps be our youngins. My name is Drew."

Cooper extended his hand and nearly winced at the power in the other's grip.

"Pleased to meet you, ma'am," he said, nodding at the woman.

She was of lighter complexion than her husband, perhaps mulatto. The children, likewise, were light-skinned, with fine, sharp features.

When the two men were seated at the table, the woman placed steaming cups of black coffee before them and turned again to her business at the small cookstove. An aroma of fried potatoes and onions filled the room, and Cooper's stomach rumbled.

"You might call it a run-in," said Drew. "Killed me one of 'em. Would of got the others too, but some haulers come along an' thought I was the bad one — opened fire on me. Had no choice but to run. Me an' them boys, the haulers, got it straightened out later, but by then the three of them was long gone. Tooken out after the girl, I reckon."

Cooper looked up. "The girl got away?"

"She did. I kept 'em pinned down whilst she ran. That's when I kilt that one. He was goin' to open up on the girl. I s'pected her to show up here — hollered at her to make for my cabin, but so far she ain't showed up."

Cooper frowned. If the girl were running around loose in the mountains, she was in trouble. As bad as the thought was, she stood to be safer with her captors for the time, until Cooper could catch up with them. Four on horseback would be easier to track than trying to pick up the trail of one small person on foot in all this snowy waste. Almost surely she was inadequately dressed. If she were still free, it would be a race between being found by either Cooper or the three remaining killers, or being brought down by the cold or starvation.

"The haulers tol' me they gathered up the horses for 'em," Drew continued. "They on horseback, her on foot, they prob'ly got her by now. Prob'ly why she ain't showed up."

Cooper sipped at the coffee. It was good. When he placed his cup on the table, his stomach again rumbled ominously.

Elizabeth, passing behind his chair at the moment, heard the quake and laid her hand on his shoulder in a motherly fashion.

"You be stayin' for supper, Marshal," she said matter-of-factly. "How long since you had you a square meal?"

Cooper grinned, embarrassed, placing a hand over his accusing belly. "It's been a spell, ma'am. And I thank you for the invitation."

Drew nodded. "You best plan on spendin' the night. It be dark in another hour anyhow. Lest you mind stayin' with colored folks."

Cooper looked quickly into the broad, black face. "I appreciate your kindness, Mr. Drew. I'd be grateful to spend the night."

CHAPTER 21

Cooper scouted the area where the clash with Drew had taken place, but it revealed nothing. The snow had virtually wiped out all trace of the passing of any souls. Cooper had gone along with the black man's thinking: likely they had recaptured the girl and were now making for Telluride.

Cooper rode for five days until he reached Telluride. The snow-covered wagon roads, the sleepless nights in the cold, took savage toll on the already weakened condition of the lawman. More than anything else, he needed rest and warmth, a good hotel bed, and lots of good, solid food.

Before checking into the hotel, he made for the sheriff's office. It and the jail were situated on the ground floor of the brick courthouse.

A slat-thin man with shirtsleeves rolled up to expose red underwear looked up from the desk as Cooper entered.

"You're not going to stand there all day lettin' the cold in, are ya?" was the caustic

165

comment as Cooper, holding onto the door-knob, scraped snow from his boots on the porch mat.

He stepped inside unhurriedly and closed the door behind him. With deliberate calm, he shrugged out of his coat and helped himself to a cup of coffee from the pot on the cherry-red stove.

When he turned around, the sheriff saw the marshal's pewter shield on his shirt, and the man's jaws, working a quid of tobacco, paused a moment. The bleary, disinterested eyes lifted to take in Cooper's face, his sunken, beard-encrusted cheeks.

"What can I do for ya, Marshal?" His tone was somewhat mollified. "I'm Sheriff Bob Peebles."

Cooper dropped without invitation into the chair before the desk. "Ben Cooper. I'm looking for three men. One girl — thirteen or fourteen years old. May have passed through here."

The sheriff resumed chewing, appearing thoughtful. "Get a lot of people running back and forth along these wagon roads, even in winter. When would they have been here?"

"Week ago. Maybe less." Cooper tasted the coffee, shuddered, and set the cup on the sheriff's desk. He would do without before he would drink that vile stuff. "Older man.

166

And a youngster, early twenties. And then one big, mean-looking one. Wears a beard, carries a blacksnake over his shoulder."

The sheriff appeared to consider a moment, while Cooper's eyes bored mildly into him. After a prolonged wait the sheriff dropped his eyes to his desk and shuffled some papers.

"I don't reckon there'd be a reward for these men?" he asked finally.

"I wouldn't know," Cooper replied wearily. "I don't even know their names. They've been doing some pretty ornery things, and I've been on their trail right along."

The sheriff nodded. "I can see you been through the mill. How much longer you think you're goin' to be able to keep after 'em?"

"Until the rooftops of hell are two feet under ice." Cooper's tone bore a hard, final line. "You seen them or not?"

The sheriff shook his head. "No. I ain't seen 'em. Like I said, folks passin' through back an' forth all the time. You'll have to check around. Livery, stores, saloons. What about the gal? How does she fit in?"

Cooper was tired — tired of this man and tired of this conversation. "They kidnapped her, after they tortured and killed her father." Cooper rose to his feet. "I'll talk to folks around town. Maybe somebody's seen them. I wouldn't want to drag you out of your nice warm office to help me, Sheriff, but I would appreciate it — if you think of anything — if you'd let me know. You can leave a message at the hotel."

He moved stiffly to the door, slipping into his coat as he went.

"There is a young girl's life at stake, if it means anything to you."

Cooper checked into the Fairmont on Telluride's main street. He took a corner room overlooking the street, climbed the stairs, and deposited his gear. After putting up the steeldust at the livery, he located a barber shop, and indulged himself with a shave and a long, leisurely soak in a hot bath. Afterward, he returned to the hotel, ate in the dining room, then climbed the stairs leadenly once more to his room.

He barely found the strength to undress. He was more exhausted than he had ever been in his life, and he examined his wasted frame in the mirror over the dresser. He gazed at his body with a hopeless expression on his haggard face. The long, ropy muscles were layered across the gaunt frame, more like flaccid binding rope than living flesh. With his ribs and shoulder blades showing through the skin, he compared his body to that of a half-starved coyote he had seen that morning.

For the hundredth time he wondered if he could, in his present condition, take on the three remaining killers with any realistic hope of coming out on top? The wound in his back, though healing, ached with a vengeance. The shirt was a constant irritation, causing intense itching in a place that was simply unreachable for a good, satisfying scratch. And there was the exhaustion, the absence of the volition to even move.

Survival instinct alone roused him to move to the door and prop a chair-back under the knob.

Laying his six-gun on the bedside stand, Cooper crawled between the sheets and experienced, as he lay back, an ecstasy he had not dreamed existed in the simple act of going to bed.

He let his eyes close of their own accord, reaching out and extinguishing the lamp with one groping hand. Sleep hit him like a gloved fist, driving him into a deep, dreamless slumber.

CHAPTER 22

They had ridden into Telluride four days before, bedraggled, hungry, riding horses with barely enough strength left to drag through the churned mud and slush.

A man at the Cosmopolitan Saloon had rented them the shack. The same man had set up an appointment for Deke to see the great man himself, Nolan.

The morning after their arrival, Deke had sold Christie's mare to the Monarch Livery Stable for a paltry sum. Considering the wasted condition of the animal, he counted himself lucky to get that. Besides, he figured that after he struck a bargain with Nolan, Christie would no longer have need for the horse. Most of the money had gone to buy Christie a new dress and a dainty pair of shoes for the appointment with Nolan. The remainder of the money went for food, and the past two days they had eaten well, Deke Chambers urging Christie to stuff herself. Fattening the calf for the slaughter, Christie had thought bitterly.

On the trail to Telluride, she had made one final attempt at escape, only to have the mare flounder in a snowbank. Unable in her weakened condition to fight through the drifts, the wasted animal had finally just laid down. When they caught her she had been whipped — not with Delwin's whip but with Papa Deke's wide leather belt, so as to not leave marks.

Thursday, the day of their appointment with Nolan, they saw Cooper ride down the mudded main street, the big man on the steeldust. Deke's eyes followed from behind the curtained window of the shack.

"What's wrong, Pa?" asked Frankie. "You gone white as a ghost."

"He's here," answered the older man through tight lips. "He followed us. Somehow he followed us all this way!"

His two sons scrambled for the window, clustered around Chambers, while Christie felt a wild surge of hope.

"Git back, ye damn fools! You want him to see you? Thanks be to God them horses be put up at the livery."

"By the same God, he don't look no better'n us," observed Delwin, peering over his father's shoulder as the lawman rode slowly past. "That hoss's been through hell."

"He's the one all right," Deke muttered

more to himself than to the others. "I know it. I can feel it."

"Why?" asked Frankie. "Why all of a sudden he shows up? He be the same one we lost back on the flats. Hell, Pa, that was weeks back. How did he find our trail again?"

Deke shook his head. "However he did it, he's here. And we might as well figure on dealin' with him. We got the advantage. He don't know what we look like. As long as we don't group together on the street, it ain't likely he'll pick us out. We'll have to keep the girl under wraps, too, until I take her over to Nolan's tonight."

"How much you goin' to ask for her?" asked Delwin, eyeing Christie with what seemed to be genuine regret.

"As much as I can." Deke turned from the window. "Enough to pay us fer all the time we got invested in her." He turned to Frankie. "I see the fella. He stopped at the sheriff's office. That settles it. He be the law. I want you to keep tabs on him, boy. Don't get too close. And don't let him spot you. We'll watch our chance and nail him when he ain't lookin'."

"I'll do it, Pa," said Delwin. "An' I'll meet him head on. I ain't scared of him."

Deke looked at Delwin evenly. "I lost one of my boys. I don't aim to lose another. We'll do it my way."

Frankie slipped into his coat and walked wordlessly out the door. He followed the lawman, first to the sheriff's office and the barber shop, then to the hotel where he sat drinking coffee while hungrily watching Cooper pack away roast beef and potatoes with gravy.

When the marshal had gone upstairs, Frankie waited a few minutes and then approached the man at the desk. A sneak glance at the open registry told him Cooper's name and credentials. By telling the desk clerk that he had a message from the sheriff for the marshal, he was able to find out Cooper's room number.

Back at the shack he passed the information on to Deke and Delwin.

"Tonight would be the best time," he advised Delwin, "after we be rid of the girl."

"Hell!" said Papa Deke. "She be most eighteen — nineteen in August!"

"Don't lie to me, Chambers," Nolan replied wearily. "She isn't over thirteen. Fourteen at best. That sheriff's not for much, but if I start pushing children he'll be on me quicker'n skunk grease. Now you take her and get the hell out of here." He strode to the door and flung it wide. "You get some full-grown merchandise and we got something to talk about."

Chambers jerked Christie's arm so sharply

173

it cracked her neck, sending shivers of pain down her spine. He stormed past Nolan, out the door, dragging the girl behind.

Once on the street, he stopped beneath a kerosene street lamp and turned on Christie angrily. "I told you how to act! You paid me no heed at all!"

Christie's eyes had been cast down, at her shoes. Now she looked up at him, a slow grin spreading her cracked lips.

"Guess you're stuck with some worthless baggage a while longer," she said, her eyes laughing at him.

He struck her a stinging blow, driving her across the plank walk against the brick building. She cracked her head against the wall, and her knees sagged. A thin trickle of blood erupted from her nose.

"You be so goddamn smart," Deke said with a smirk. "I guess there's nothing left but to marry you off to Delwin." He smiled at her alarm. "An' we be doin' that this very night, missy."

He grabbed her arm and dragged her along the walk toward the tarpaper shack.

Delwin needed a drink. His palms were sticky and his mouth was cotton. In spite of his bravado with his pa and Frankie, his swaggering before Christie, he much preferred facing helpless victims. That the marshal was a formidable man was evidenced by his showing up, still on their trail after all this time.

The Cosmopolitan was crowded: miners mostly, and haulers, and the inevitable hangers-on — gamblers and prostitutes. Delwin moved to the bar — the tables were filled — and looked hungrily at the women in their bawdy finery. If only he had the money, he pined. Maybe after Christie was sold, he could . . .

"What'll it be, mister?" The bartender was a large black man with a wide, friendly face and enormous hands. Delwin looked up, startled for a moment, recalling his last encounter with a large black man. He grinned, relaxed. It was not the same man, obviously.

"How much for a shot?" he asked, reaching a fist into his pocket.

"Two bits," replied the bartender. Then he added jokingly, "Or we can give you our first-timer's special — twenty-five cents."

Smart ass, Delwin thought as his hand closed around the coins in his pocket. He opened his hand and counted out the twenty-five cents in change. Two gray lead pennies remained in his hand when he was finished.

The bartender set a polished glass on the counter, dolloped a shot expertly from an open bottle. "There you go, big-spender," he said with a sly smile, and moved off to the other end of the bar.

Delwin scowled, but he took the whiskey. He sipped gratefully, inhaling and savoring its burning, comforting fire.

As he nursed his drink, his eyes roamed about the room, dwelling on the gaming tables, on the nude painting on the far wall, and, again, on the women, laughing and talking loudly with the men at the tables.

He stood with his back at the bar, elbows resting on the polished wood.

A woman sat at the nearest table in a chair facing him, watching three men in rough-looking work clothes gambling and paying her little mind. Beneath the layers of makeup, she bore a plain face, slightly horsey, but her eyes were friendly and when Delwin grinned stupidly at her, she smiled back and raised her glass in a friendly salute.

She got up slowly and walked to the bar, her silken skirts rustling. She stopped next to him, deliciously close, and waves of her strong perfume washed over him, confusing him, tying his tongue up in knots. Her shoulders were bare, white, and rounded. Two narrow straps held the low-cut dress above her ample breasts. She stood with a whimsical smile while Delwin drank her in.

Finally he found his tongue. "Well, now,"

he began smoothly, "if you ain't a sight fer sore eyes."

She ran her long fingers through her rich red hair, then held up her empty glass. "If you're any good with that whip, let's see if you can whip us up a couple of drinks. I know where there's an empty table." She smiled seductively and reached out one pale hand and stroked the ever-present whip coiled over his left shoulder.

Delwin looked into green eyes, placed his glass to his lips with fingers lightly trembling, and polished off his drink in one swallow.

He turned toward the bar and his arm circled naturally around the girl's bare shoulders. Just as naturally, her own right arm encircled his waist.

"Lucky Charley," she called to the black bartender. "That'll be two more, for my friend and me." Her voice was low and smoky, and Delwin could imagine it whispering low in his ear, red lips pressed close.

The bartender moved up slowly, a look of bored resignation on his broad face.

"You got you a bum steer in this one, Norma," he said, jerking a thumb at Delwin. "I just took his last nickel." He made a careless swipe at the bar top with a damp rag.

A flush mounted Delwin's neck and crept up beneath his thick beard.

"Now how do you expect to entertain a lady without no money?" she asked with a laugh, then squeezed him playfully around his waist.

Delwin looked murderously at the bartender. "I got money," he challenged. "Back at the hotel. Give us a couple on the tab, and then I'll run over an' get some."

"C'mon, Lucky," pleaded the girl with a wink at Delwin. "Set him up for one round. He's good for it."

"You know the rules, Norma," the bartender said flatly. He tossed the towel to the back bar and placed huge, meaty arms on the bar. "I don't work for nothin', and neither do you."

The girl shrugged her lovely shoulders and turned her smiling face up to Delwin.

"Sorry, sugar. The man's right. Rules is rules." Her arm dropped from his waist as she slipped from beneath his arm; she walked back to the table without a backward glance.

Rage numbed Delwin's tongue, and his fists clenched in useless fury.

"Sorry, pal," the bartender said, slapping the bar with a palm, like a judge declaring sentence. Lucky turned smiling to the back bar and the stack of glasses awaiting his polishing touch.

A leather loop dropped about Lucky's neck, and he was dragged backward and draped across the bar. He clawed at the thing across his throat.

"Hey!" someone shouted. "He's got Lucky! The bastard's killin' Lucky!"

A score of burly miners and teamsters leaped to their feet in a confusing, stumbling flurry. They surged about Delwin and his victim. Rough hands clasped Delwin's shirt and beard, ripping, pulling him free from the whip and from the bartender.

Lucky's eyes bulged, and his swollen, purplish tongue protruded.

Delwin, jerked backward, toppled and fell to the floor. A half-dozen dust-covered bodies fell upon him, punching, gouging, suffocating. Delwin managed a scream. Someone had bitten him on the nose, hard enough that blood coursed down his cheeks and neck.

It was a circus. Those not involved in the melee stood and watched and shouted encouragement and advice to those rolling about and grappling on the sawdust-strewn floor. The saloon shook with raucous laughter. One of the women lifted her skirts, exposing silken bloomers, and clambered first to a tabletop, then to the shoulders of the nearest man, the better to see the action.

Lucky clung to the bar, eyes red, bleeding from the nostrils, gasping air as though drowning.

"We got the bastard," shouted one of the men from the tangle on the floor. "What do ya want to do with him, Luck?"

Lucky gulped, his face twisted in rage. His first attempt to speak was a gurgle. "Hang the sonofabitch," he ordered in a whisper.

A silence like a curtain fell over the room. Delwin, subdued, lay pressed beneath the bodies of four stout men. He seemed stunned. He was in serious trouble, and he knew it. His mind, sluggish on its best days, now refused to work altogether. Animal panic mounted, took control, and he trembled all over.

"Well, why the hell not?" put in the woman seated on the teamster's shoulders. "He damn near killed Lucky, didn't he?"

A chorus of yells rocked the glasses in the back bar.

"Take him outside," said one of the miners. "I know just the spot."

Rough hands jerked Delwin to his feet. He was pressed in a mob of drunken, angry men and women.

His gunbelt was stripped from him, and his hands were jerked sharply behind his back and bound with his own bullwhip.

"I didn't mean nothin'," he moaned to unsympathetic ears. "Let me go. I was jus' leavin' town. I'll go right now!"

"I just bet you would, you sonofabitch," said the woman astride the man's shoulders. Her eyes were wild with excitement.

The troop moved en masse toward the door, dragging Delwin by his arms. His legs had suddenly refused to hold him up.

Sparse islands of light from kerosene lanterns on poles guttered in the blackness. Across the street from the Cosmopolitan stood one of the main street's lampposts. The crowd burst through the doors and surged toward the sickly yellow light, dragging Delwin, moaning and cursing, through the muck.

A lariat was produced, and one end was tossed over the metal arm supporting the lamp. The loop dropped to dangle horribly before Delwin's bulging eyes. At that point he lost control and wet himself.

"Bring that hoss over here," ordered Lucky, who, regaining his voice, had entered fully into the spirit of the moment.

No time was taken to fashion a hangman's noose. It was to be a strangulation-type hanging, using the sliding loop already in the lariat. Rough hands hoisted Delwin atop the horse, and the rope settled unceremoniously about his neck, where it was pulled snug and tied off on the base of the lamppost.

Delwin's eyes seemed about to burst from his skull. A portion of his beard was caught beneath the rope, holding his mouth agape. Already the taut rope had cut off his protests. At this point he had become a silent spectator to his own hanging.

His frantic eyes caught the glint of a badge among the crowd. The sheriff stood on the boardwalk, arms folded, gazing placidly, a fixed smile on his lips.

Delwin twisted his neck violently, fighting for slack in the noose and air space. His eyes bore pleadingly into those of the sheriff.

"Relax, boy," the sheriff called out calmly. "They're just hoo-rahin' ya. They ain't actually going to hang ya. Right, boys?"

Lucky chose that moment to slap the bay horse on the rump, sending it charging down the street.

It began in Cooper's mind as the angry drone of hornets working like stingers into his fogged brain and senses. Gunfire brought him out of his sleep, back to the cheerless, icy room in the hotel.

He crawled, fully clothed, from the blankets and stumbled, six-gun in hand, to the window.

The scene below was a carnival, men firing their guns into the air, dancing about in the mud of the street. At the center of the mob, legs thrashing like a windmill, a man spun on the end of a rope fixed on a lamppost.

Cooper tried without success to raise the window. It was painted shut. Reluctantly, thinking of the additional cold that would invade his frigid room, he picked up a chair and threw it through the glass.

All eyes turned upward at the crash, looked uneasily at the man in the window with the six-gun pointed into the crowd.

"Loosen the rope," he shouted, quieting the last of the crowd.

"Who the hell are you?" Lucky challenged. "This man near killed me. He deserves to hang."

"A jury will have to decide that. Let him down, I said."

No one moved. Delwin continued to thrash at the end of the rope. His face was approaching deep purple in hue. His swollen tongue lolled horribly from his mouth.

"Sheriff," called Cooper from the window, "if that man dies, I'm arresting you for murder."

The sheriff blinked, then shrugged and walked to the lamppost. He jerked the end of the rope, unraveling the slip knot, dumping Delwin Chambers with a dull splat into the sea of icy mud.

"Fellas just having a little fun, Marshal," the sheriff called up to the broken window.

At the mention of Cooper's authority a ripple of wonder ran through the crowd. Several began to wander away, some pausing and looking back to get a better glimpse of the mystery lawman in the hotel window.

Delwin lay where he had landed, apparently forgotten by the crowd. With the rope about his neck now slack, color was returning to his face. He lay with one eye in the muck, groaning senselessly and struggling with the whip binding his hands behind him.

A toe dug into his ribs, prodding painfully.

"On yer feet, bad man," said the sheriff. "You ain't hurt none." He grabbed the handle of the whip and pulled Delwin, whimpering and moaning, to his knees. The mud and ooze clung to his face and beard, and he looked around him in frightened wonder. It was true — he was alive. A sob of relief escaped him.

Delwin looked up as the tall, broad form of Ben Cooper came out of the hotel and slogged through the mud to his side.

Without preliminaries, Cooper said, "I'm filing a report with the district federal judge on your conduct here tonight, Sheriff. I've never seen a duly sworn lawman take part in a mob lynching before —"

He paused, considering the whip binding Delwin's hands.

"Do you know this man?" Cooper asked

abruptly, grasping Delwin by the arms and pulling him to his feet.

Delwin gave Cooper one baleful glance and averted his eyes toward the mud.

"Never laid eyes on him," answered the sheriff. His tone was surly. "Not until tonight."

A teamster, one of the few remaining spectators, coiling up the rope which had nearly ended Delwin's life, commented, "The sorry sonofabitch tried to strangle Lucky with that goddamn whip."

Cooper unraveled the whip from around Delwin's wrists. He looked at the coiled, braided leather closely.

"Why did you think the man deserved strangling?" Cooper eyed Delwin.

Chambers ran his fingers through his caked and filthy beard. His eyes were furtive and he avoided looking at Cooper.

The teamster spoke up again. "Him an' Lucky got into it on account this fella here wanted drinks fer hisself and one of the girls and he didn't have no money to pay. Lucky tol' him to leave an' this fella throws a loop around Lucky's neck."

Cooper listened without comment, quickly assessing the situation and his next move.

"Don't make this bigger'n it is, Marshal," said the sheriff. "Lucky an' the man jus' had

a misunderstandin'. Fella lost his head —
didn't really mean to hurt Lucky. An' the
crowd was just havin' fun. They weren't really
goin' to hang him."

"Could've fooled me," grumbled Delwin,
rubbing angry rope burns on his whiskered
neck.

"What's your name?"

"Chambers." He had tried desperately to
think of another name, any name, but abso-
lutely nothing occurred to him.

Cooper coiled the whip and handed it to
Chambers. "Well, Chambers, how about it?
You want to press charges against anyone?
You got that right. Course that fella *you* tried
to strangle could bring charges against you
as well."

Delwin clutched the whip. He shook his
head. "I just wanna get the hell away from
here. You people are crazy." He turned to
leave.

"You staying someplace close?" Cooper
asked. As he spoke, a shudder passed through
the marshal's frame. He had left the room
without a coat and he was starting to chill
again.

"Me an' my family, we got us a little shack
south o' town."

"What're you doing in Telluride?" There
was a curious edge to Cooper's voice that

186

caused the sheriff to suddenly look up and pay attention.

"I be lookin' fer a job, Marshal. Anything wrong with that?"

Cooper reached out a hand and again took the whip from Chambers, on the pretext of examining its workmanship.

"A skinner, huh? Ought to be a lot of jobs open for drivers around these parts. Course, I don't know that for sure," Cooper explained. "Just got to town myself. Come up from the flats." He was looking intently at Chambers. "I'm on the trail of three men. They made off with a girl."

The sheriff's attention was focused on Delwin.

"That's got nothin' to do with me, Marshal. Me an' my family, we come from Ouray. Before that, we been in New Mexico."

"You were doin' some haulin' in Ouray, were you?" asked the sheriff.

"Sure thing," Delwin reached out a timid hand, taking his whip almost shyly from the marshal. "Well, if that be all . . ."

"Who did you drive for in Ouray?" asked the sheriff. "What was the name of the outfit?"

"The Honeybee Line," answered Delwin without hesitation. "Weather got so bad up that way they had to shut down for a time. Laid off a bunch of us fellas. I come down to Telluride to see if I can scrape me up somethin' to tide me over." He had sensed the sheriff's ploy and had dodged it neatly. In the Cosmopolitan Saloon earlier he had overheard a man mention the Honeybee Freightline and its closing because of the weather.

The sheriff seemed satisfied and pursued it no further.

"All right, Chambers," Cooper said. "Good luck to you and your family."

Delwin waved and turned away.

They watched as Delwin slogged away through the mud, never looking back. His stride was purposeful, almost hurried.

"I'm going to my room and get my coat," Cooper said, watching the retreating form. "Follow him. I want to know where it is he and his family are staying. I'll meet you back at your office."

A pained expression worked the sheriff's narrow jaw. "Well now, it seems, Marshal, that I might be adoin' yer job. I got my own job to think about."

Cooper turned on him, a cold light in his eyes. "If it's your job you're thinking about, you best be doing what I tell you. In case you forgot, Sheriff, I caught you in a gross dereliction of duty. Your cooperation might just determine how I handle that little matter."

Cooper turned and walked toward the hotel, followed by the sheriff's murderous glare.

Thirty minutes later he sat in the sheriff's office, at Peebles's desk. Though it was warm in the small room, Cooper sat bundled in his coat. He looked wan and gaunt and badly in need of sleep. He had wondered, hopefully, if the nightmare might be nearly over, and now, as the sheriff entered and stomped mud from his boots, Cooper looked up hopefully.

"It was just like the man said," intoned Peebles flatly. "They got 'em a shack at the edge of town — old tarpaper affair — next to the Batwing Mine."

Cooper nodded. "I know the place. Spotted it when I rode in."

Peebles poured himself a cup of coffee, held up the pot, and looked inquiringly at Cooper. Cooper shook his head. He shivered slightly.

"Wasn't much light in the place," the sheriff said, taking a chair opposite the marshal. "Couldn't see how many were inside. And I couldn't get too close — weren't no cover." He looked closely at the marshal. "You don't look so good. If these are the people you're after, are you going to be able to handle 'em — in your condition?"

Cooper looked up, "I'll handle them, all right. Besides, I'll have your help." He pulled

189

his six-gun from under his coat and checked its loads.

The sheriff sighed resignedly. "I still can't figure how I got roped into this dance. We ought to wait until daylight and get us a few more men. The shack sets up against the bank. We could fill it with lead until nothing moved, and then just walk in with shovels and buckets."

"You're forgetting the girl," said Cooper impatiently. "If she's still alive and still with them, I don't want her buying a stray bullet." He slipped the six-gun back into its holster. "We'll do it my way," he said evenly. "I'll give them a half-hour to get settled, then we'll move in."

CHAPTER 23

They approached the cabin on foot, stepping lightly in the dark. There was, as the sheriff had said, no cover. The shack stood isolated against the rock bank, a sickly yellow light showing through the curtained windows.

Cooper moved to one side of the cabin and crouched at one of the windows. Peebles stood at the opposite corner, stationed there by the marshal so that he could cover both the front of the cabin and the side opposite from where Cooper stood.

Cooper waited several moments, listening. There was no sound from within.

In the dark, Cooper frowned. Something didn't feel right. He paused, uncertain. Drawing his six-gun, he eased himself softly into a position where he could see into the dimly glowing room.

He made out two muffled forms on bunks against the wall, two more shrouded figures on the floor.

He hunkered low, passing beneath the window, and moved to the front of the shack.

Peebles appeared startled, gun raised. When he recognized the marshal, he gave an almost audible sigh and shook his head grimly.

Avoiding the two windows across the front of the shack, Cooper soft-stepped to where the anxious sheriff waited.

"Quiet as a tomb inside," he informed Peebles. "Looks like they're all asleep. But it could be a trap. Be on your toes."

They moved to the door, guns drawn. The night air had become hushed, strained, as though a thousand ears awaited the next sound.

Standing to the right of the door, Cooper laid an ear against the rough plank. Suddenly he stepped back, launched one foot to strike the door just below the knob.

The door exploded inward and the two men stepped quickly inside, guns leveled.

The forms on the bunk beds, the two blanketed forms on the floor did not move.

"Damn," muttered Cooper. He kicked at one of the sleeping figures on the floor. Blankets and something dry and crackling went flying.

"Corn husks," said Peebles. He watched as Cooper tore the blankets and tarps from the bunks. "The bastards stuffed their beds with corn husks. Tore up somebody's mattress, I warrant."

"I'll be goddamn," said Cooper, his voice tight with anger. "He must've made you when you followed him."

"Hell he did!" defended Peebles. "I stayed way back — just barely kept him in sight."

Cooper looked about helplessly. In his hand he still held the six-gun. "Nothing!" he choked. "Nothing. They've cleared out."

Peebles looked at him with concern. The lawman was trembling, anger and frustration on his face. He looked to be near the point of attacking anything close at hand.

The sheriff was the first to see the note. It was propped up on the table beneath the soot-blackened lamp. With an anxious glance at the marshal, he retrieved the wrinkled bit of paper, held it close to the lamp.

"What have you got?" Cooper demanded. He thrust his six-gun into the holster and took the note from Peebles.

The sheriff gave a dry chuckle. "Least they thought enough of you to leave a forwarding address."

Cooper gave the man a scorn-filled glance and held the note to the light. The yellow paper trembled in his fingers:

Lawman — we be a mined to tok a deel. For $100. dolars we be given the gurl to u. we be moovin east. u do not folow.

Brang 100 to cole min columbin north of town midnite tomaro or gurl dies.

S. D. Chambers

Cooper balled the paper in his fist and threw it across the room.

"He means the Columbine," Peebles said. "'Bout a mile north of Telluride. It's a shutdown coal mine. Been closed for years."

A small woodstove stood in one corner. Without warning Cooper drew his six-gun and fired five rounds as rapidly as he could pull the trigger. The .45 bucked in his hand, and the slugs tore through the cast-iron sides of the stove. Soot exploded from the cracks around the stove lids and from the pipe through the roof. The stove's small door with glass windows was flung wide.

Peebles backed uneasily toward the door.

Cooper jammed fresh rounds into his gun, holstered it, then walked over to the bunks lined against the wall. With almost deliberate calm he smashed the wooden frames, tore the upright supports from the floor.

Then, with a short length of two-by-four, he smashed all the windows and tore loose the ragged curtains. Peebles slipped out the door.

When Cooper finished, the room was in shambles. He stood by the door, hat far back on his head, forehead gleaming with sweat.

Cooper stood for a minute, surveying his work, his chest rising and falling as though he had just wrestled a calf to the ground. He seemed satisfied at last. But one final touch was needed.

He walked to the rickety table — the one remaining intact piece of furniture in the room — seized the kerosene lamp, and threw it against the far wall, exploding the glass.

The flames flowed with the oil, a thousand tongues of orange and blue, licking at the tinder-dry floor and walls.

In less than a minute the fire was beyond stopping. The room was filled with a terrific heat, choking smoke, and the ancient wood popping and cracking like fireworks.

Finally Cooper walked from the shack, not looking back. He walked directly by the sheriff. He did not so much as glance at the man. He did not speak.

He moved swiftly to where the horses were tied and mounted the steeldust. The exploding flames behind him were reflected in the horse's wide, frightened eyes.

Peebles mounted his own horse and spurred the animal to overtake the steeldust.

"You can get the money from the bank, Marshal," Peebles said. In his tone was a new respect. Gone was his insolent indifference.

He had witnessed the transformation of this placid man into a destructive beast, and the mild sheriff had no desire to taste the wrath of that beast.

"We can get the money first thing in the morning," the sheriff offered again. "By midnight tomorrow it'll all be over."

Cooper did not look at the sheriff when he spoke, but his meaning was deadly.

"I've been trailing these bastards all over the Southwest, Peebles. I'm tired of it. I'm tired of all this bullshit."

"But the money —"

"To hell with the money. For all the bodies they've left behind and all the evil they put me and that girl through, I'll pay them bastards in a coin they won't forget."

CHAPTER 24

A rope had been tied off to an overhead beam in the mouth of the mine. An empty coal car stood at the entrance. A short wooden plank had been laid across the top of the car, from side to side. Standing upon the plank, her hands tied behind her back, was Christie. The rope from the beam ended in a noose about her neck.

All eventualities had been covered. Poised as it was with the brake off, a single nudge, even a pistol shot fired into the car, could begin it moving along the narrow-gauge track, leaving Christie dangling in midair. There was no way to reach her, to remove the noose, without traversing the open area in front of the mine, exposing oneself almost surely to deadly gunfire.

Cooper and Peebles pushed their horses down off the sharp embankment and onto the wagon road. The horses' hooves struck sparks on the rocky roadbed. At the sound, the two faces staring into the fire glanced up, then looked at one another.

The open area was bathed in soft moonlight, and Cooper recognized immediately the form of Delwin Chambers.

As the two lawmen rode up to the fire Cooper looked directly at Delwin. "I should have let them hang you."

Delwin grinned and scratched his beard thoughtfully. "I never did thank you, Marshal. My bacon was gettin' a mite crisp on the ends when you showed up. An', like you can see, it give us a pretty good idea." He jerked a thumb at Christie, standing silent on the makeshift scaffold.

"I don't need to tell you, Marshal," said Deke, "if you ever done any mining, just how easy them cars roll once they been started. Be ye understandin', one move we don't like, and little Frankie, my youngest, gives a yank on that old car and sends Christie down the rails to perdition. Are we clear on that score, Marshal?"

"Couldn't be plainer," said Cooper easily. He looked from Deke to Delwin. "Would I be right in guessing this one's your son, too?"

"You'd be right. We're the Chambers clan. Samuel Deke Chambers, at your service."

"I seem to recall," continued Cooper casually, "you started out with three sons. Something happen to one along the way?"

"You know goddamn good an' well what happened to my boy!" exploded Chambers. "That nigger killed 'im. Back shot Lance — give 'im no chance at all." He spat savagely into the flames, and the look he directed at Cooper was murderous.

Cooper glanced casually at Christie. He was playing for time. He had guessed there might be someone planted in the tunnel, close to the girl. And he would be hidden behind the coal car, safe from being picked off with a desperate shot.

Cooper shot a quick glance at Peebles who looked at the cave, back at the marshal, and then shrugged his shoulders helplessly.

Chambers chuckled, "Oh, he's there all right." He turned and called out in the direction of the mine. "Frankie, without givin' 'em a target, stick somethin' out so's they can see ya."

After a moment a small hand flourishing a white handkerchief appeared around the end of the coal car.

"That's enough, Frankie," called Chambers. "They see ya." He turned to the marshal. "Well, did ya bring the money?"

Cooper smiled openly. "Of course. And it's yours just as soon as you get the gal down off that car and turn her over to me."

Again Deke laughed, in a mirthless way.

"You'd sooner talk us all out of our guns, Marshal — or our underwear. Soon's I get the money in hand, you get the girl. You stall around, an' she's like to die. She's been standin' on that plank for the last half-hour. And in case you ain't paid attention, those spindly little legs of hers are startin' to wobble a mite. She slips off'n that plank an' it's all over." His features turned grim. "Now I suggest we get this business over with in a timely manner. An' we can all be on our way."

In the coals of the campfire sat a blackened coffeepot. Cooper picked up a tin cup and poured it full. He took a sip and made a face. His entire manner was calm, nearly indifferent. After seeing Frankie's hand from behind the coal car, Cooper restrained himself from even glancing in the direction of the girl.

The marshal turned to Peebles. "Sheriff, I want you to try a cup of this," he said, indicating the coffee. "At least then you'll be able to say you found somebody that could make coffee worse than yours. This is the most vile stuff I ever tasted. You could soak fence posts in this and they'd never rot."

Cooper was stalling, and it was painfully obvious not only to the sheriff but to the outlaws as well.

"You weren't invited out here in the middle

of the night to drink coffee," said Delwin. "Pa, he's killin' time."

"I be warnin' you, Marshal," said the elder Chambers. "You be playin' with that gal's life. Once that plank goes, it's too late fer any negotiations."

Cooper took another sip of the coffee. He replied, "That might be a good thing for you to keep in mind yourself. Look at it this way, we ain't payin' for a dead horse. If that girl dies, there's nothing to keep us from blasting you apart."

"Nothin' 'cept me, my boys, an' our guns. We got us a purt-near stalemate. An' that ain't even countin' Frankie's Winchester there in the cave. An' when the shootin's all done, we still take the hundred dollars off yer corpses."

"A hundred dollars." Cooper laughed softly. "All this running and hiding, the cold and wet, just barely scraping by — all for a lousy hundred dollars. Somehow it just don't seem like good business."

"It's a start for us, Marshal. We had figured on a lot more, that's true. Ol' Hap Hinkle was a hell of a highwayman in his day. And it would stand to reason he'd leave some of the loot stashed somewheres — for the girl's sake, if nothin' else."

"You're so sure he didn't?" questioned Cooper, his mind racing while he stalled, searching for the edge, the opening.

"Oh, he would of tol' us," said Delwin with a satisfied chuckle. "We done worked that ol' man good — didn't we, Pa?"

"Also, if there'd been money put by, he'd a told the girl," said Deke. "An' I'd swear on my dead mama's forehead that gal don't know nothin' about no money."

"Did you *work* her good too?" asked Peebles, making no effort to cover the sarcasm in his tone.

"Hell no," said Delwin, stroking the whip coiled over his shoulder. "Nobody would buy damaged goods."

"So you figured," ventured Peebles, "that even without the old man's loot, if you had the girl you could always get somethin' for her? Is that about right?"

"About," answered Delwin smugly. And then a shadow of sadness settled upon his features. "'Cept Nolan wouldn't have nothin' to do with her. Too young."

Deke looked at his son, pity and impatience struggling for control in the small, black eyes. "Shut up, Delwin," he said softly. "Just shut up, huh?"

Deke Chambers turned back to the marshal. "For one hundred dollars you get the girl, you ride out of here an' leave us be. Tomorrow morning we head east to Denver. We take a boat down the Platte to St. Louis, or somewheres where we can start over. How about it, Marshal?"

"You're going to do all this on a hundred dollars?" asked Cooper wearily.

It seemed to Peebles the marshal had abandoned much of his concern for the welfare of the girl. Neither lawman, in fact, had even bothered in the last few moments to look at the girl where she stood upon her perch in the entrance of the mine.

In fact, neither had Deke nor his son. Had they looked at her, they might have seen Christie struggling to free herself from the cords binding her wrists. As unobtrusively as she could, she maneuvered her arms, stretching the fibers of her bonds a fraction of an inch at a time. If the lawmen were to rescue her, she must be ready. The marshal and the other man would have their hands full out there. Papa Deke had an ace in the hole — Frankie. And it would be up to Christie to deal with him. If it came to a shoot-out, the marshal would scarcely have time to consider her predicament, at least not until it was too late.

She pulled at the cords until sweat beaded her forehead and her arms trembled with fatigue. The effort she made must be silent and in no way alarm Frankie to her intentions.

She angled her body slightly on the plank to where she could look behind her and check on Frankie.

"You keep dancin' around on that board an' you're liable to fall on your ass," said Frankie.

Her glance showed the youngest of the killers preoccupied with the meeting of the four around the fire.

"What the hell's takin' so long?" Frankie groused. He envied them the fire and the hot coffee. And he was tired; he wanted to go to bed.

But what really picked at Frankie was the transaction itself. He felt as did Delwin, that a hundred dollars was too great a comedown from their lofty plans of the beginning. But to argue would have been pointless. Their pa was not one to subject himself to debate with his sons. Lance had been the only one of the boys to ever take a stand against him. And now Lance was dead, as surely as though the Almighty Himself had taken exception to Lance's defiance of Deke Chambers. To Frankie it was an all too likely concept. On a thousand occasions he had heard his father invoke the name of the Holy One when passing judgment on one or another of their helpless victims. It seemed at the time to lend to their doings an almost holy aura.

At the moment, however, Frankie was feeling little reverence for anything. He had been too long cold and hungry, and — he looked down upon his once-fine Navajo moccasins, now tattered and held together with straps of rawhide — he had been too long too poor.

He leaned his head wearily against the cold metal of the coal car. "God, I'm tired," he muttered.

Christie chose that instant to slip one hand free of the ropes binding her wrists.

Suppressing an impulse to jerk the noose from about her neck, she instead held her arms rigid, in the bound position. She was now ready to do her part, whenever the action started.

Delwin jerked his six-gun up and shot Sheriff Peebles in the chest. Peebles dropped like a stone.

"Ye lyin' bastards!" shrieked Papa Deke, groping for his weapon. "Ye never brought no money no how!"

His last words were drowned by the roar of Cooper's .45. Delwin, smoking gun in hand, took the marshal's bullet in the throat. The outlaw staggered backward, arms windmilling for balance. When he finally fell upon his back, he was dead.

Deke stared, dazed, his own gun forgotten in his fist.

"You . . . killed my son . . ." He looked at Cooper with shock in his eyes.

Before he could raise his gun, Cooper reached out with his left hand and jerked the weapon from his grip.

Chambers's jaw dropped. He made a lunge to grapple with the marshal, to wrest back his six-gun.

Cooper swung the outlaw's own six-gun about and pulled the trigger. The bullet took the old man in the stomach, passing through and shattering the spine. Chambers dropped in his tracks.

Frankie had been unable to fire for fear of hitting his father. When he saw the elder Chambers felled like an ox, it left the marshal the only one remaining on his feet. Frankie brought his rifle to his shoulder and took aim. It was then Christie made her move.

The cords dropped from her wrists. She tore off the noose from her neck, turned like a cat on the narrow plank and kicked Frankie full in the face.

Frankie let out a howl, dropped the rifle and put his hands to his face.

The girl dropped into the bottom of the coal car, grasped the short plank like a baseball bat, and swung it with all her young strength.

It struck Frankie a glancing blow, bouncing off his shoulder before colliding with the top of his head.

Frankie's howling ceased abruptly. He staggered backward and collided with the wall before his knees gave out and he collapsed in a heap, legs draped across the narrow-gauge tracks.

"Marshal! I got him!" came Christie's jubilant cry. "I got him!" Her voice ended in a little half-sob, and she clambered over the side of the coal car and dropped to the ground.

When Cooper reached the mine opening, she was standing over Frankie, aiming his own rifle at the unconscious outlaw's head. "They was going to hang me, Marshal. They killed Hap, they dragged me all over the country, and then they was going to hang me."

Her lower lip began to quiver. Her eyes were wide and round, and they filled with tears. "Am I safe now, Marshal? Am I rescued?" The tears spilled down her dirty cheeks.

He took the rifle and said, pulling her to his chest, "It's over now, little gal. It's over."

She collapsed weeping against him.

CHAPTER 25

There was a deputy in town, of sorts: a sleepy-eyed relaxed boy in his early twenties. Cooper deposited Frankie in a cell and seated the girl in the chair at the sheriff's desk.

He placed in her hand a cup of coffee and looked her over with concern while the girl sipped.

"Go ahead," he said gently. "Drink it. It'll perk you up." He turned to the gawking, tow-headed deputy. "Go get your doc. I want her checked over."

"What about the sheriff?" the boy asked. "Does he know what the hell's goin' on?"

"He's dead, along with the father and brother of that sonofabitch you got locked up back there."

"The sheriff's dead?" The young man's eyes widened with amazement. "Why, who's gonna keep the law in Telluride now?"

"I guess you will. You're over twenty-one, aren't you? You can use the gun, can't you?"

"Hell, no!" expostulated the young man.

208

"Only used it plinkin' varmints."

"Well, there you have it," Cooper answered with a conspiratorial wink at the pale, exhausted girl. "That's exactly what I use my gun for — shooting varmints."

The cup trembled in Christie's hands. Living with the threat of death, of being molested, or left to die of starvation had sapped the last of her inner strength. The final conflict, her battle with Frankie, had completed the process. Her wellspring of nerve and courage had run dry. The tin cup slipped from her fingers and clattered across the floor, and the young girl began to shake like a dry leaf in the wind. Her lips parted in a voiceless, sobbing wail, and she looked up at the marshal with terror-stricken eyes.

"What's happenin'?" asked the deputy, glancing nervously over his shoulder, searching for the threat that had set the girl off. "Did she catch a bullet? I didn't see no blood."

Cooper didn't answer. He took the girl in his arms and held her, while sobs wracked her thin wasted frame like blows from a fist. For several minutes the scene remained unchanged: the girl in the man's arms; the young, red-faced deputy gawking awkwardly, shifting his embarrassed gaze to the floor.

"It was horrible," she finally managed to blurt out against the marshal's chest. "What they did to Hap . . ." She clung to Cooper fiercely. "They burned him . . . they . . ."

"Hush," said Cooper softly. "Hush it up, gal. It's all over. You're safe and you're alive."

"Those lousy bastards!" the deputy shouted. "What leads a person to do somethin' like 'at to another human bein'?"

Christie pushed suddenly away from Cooper's embrace and looked up with red, angry eyes. "They was after money!" she declared savagely. "They said they knew he had gold hidden, stashed away from when he robbed stages. They tortured him to make him tell. An' then when he was dead they was going to torture me, an . . . use me. But Lance, he talked them out of it. He said maybe they could use me for ransom or somethin' — " Her chin trembled, and the tears gushed hotly.

"The lousy bastards," repeated the deputy. "That last one didn't save nothin' by comin' out of the fracas alive. He's gonna hang legal or I'll lynch him myself."

Cooper pulled the girl gently to her feet. "I'm taking you over to the hotel. After the doc looks you over I want you to sleep until at least noon tomorrow." He smiled reassuringly, slipped off his coat, and wrapped it about her thin shoulders.

"Are you hungry?"

She nodded. "Yeah. But I'm more tired.

I feel real worn out." She swayed uncertainly and looked up at Cooper with sad eyes lined with dark, blue-black circles. Her cheeks were hollow, emaciated.

The deputy suddenly spoke up. "I'll take her over to the hotel for you, Marshal. I got to go an' see about gettin' them dead men picked up anyways."

"Sounds fine," said Cooper. "Put her up in my room. No. Second thought, the window's busted. Wake the clerk up and have him fix her up with a new room. I'll bunk here in one of your cells and keep an eye on young Chambers."

He watched the sleeping prisoner for several minutes with his own head resting wearily against the bars.

A ruthless killer, rapist, scavenger . . . what else? And yet, lying there, sleeping like an innocent child.

Cooper shook his head and walked leadenly to an empty cell and threw himself across the bunk. It was cold in the cell, and he just managed to pull the woolen blanket across his long body before sleep came.

As his thoughts blurred and his mind wound down, it came to him that it was over. But now, what of the girl? What was to become of her? His last thought of the scrawny, blond waif was the first image in a very short dream that led him into a deep, exhausted, mindless slumber.

When Cooper awoke in the early morning light, Frankie was dead. During the night, he hanged himself with his heavy woolen blanket. Frankie's bulging eyes were fixed open, protruding from his effeminate-looking face.

The marshal sat up on the edge of his bunk and rubbed the night fuzz from his eyes. In a way, he was not surprised. Frankie had chosen the easier way over the wait for a trial and the jury's verdict. The end result would have been the same. Cooper felt no regret, although Frankie's death might prompt one or two to question how it could have happened with the marshal sleeping in the next cell.

It was the young deputy who was the more heavily jolted; a rock taken between the eyes could not have fazed him more.

"My God," he moaned. "Isn't this ever goin' to quit? I just got the sheriff an' this guy's pa an' brother laid out. Now I gotta go through the rigmarole all over again." He sat down heavily at the desk. While Cooper had slept, the deputy had been busy throughout the night.

"By the way," the deputy said, passing a weary hand across his forehead and pushing his hat to the back of his blond head. "I sent them telegrams to Pueblo like you asked. Here's the answer." He held across a slip of yellow paper. "Says they'll send a deputy marshal up here to look after things until the town can hold a special election for a new sheriff. I'm to be in charge until the marshal gets here."

"What I've seen so far," said Cooper, pouring from the enamel pot a cup of the deputy's coffee, "they might just as well make you in charge permanent. You seem to know how to get the job done."

The deputy looked thoughtful. "Hell, I could never be sheriff by myself. I got too much to learn yet."

"Best way to learn it is on the job." Cooper gingerly tried the coffee. It was good. "You got a good start on it already," he said. "Coffee's a hell of a lot better than that stuff Peebles had in the pot."

CHAPTER 26

Even the steeldust felt better, high-stepping through the muck in the wheel ruts as they made their way down the slope. They passed beneath the high-reaching pines, drifts of brown snow piled on either side of the road. They rode, one in either wheel track, the girl and Cooper, with the bay packhorse tied in behind the lawman.

The two days spent resting in Telluride had done the girl nearly as much good as it had Cooper. Her pale cheeks had colored, even began to fill out a bit. Blond curly hair, clean and combed, fresh new clothes, she looked every bit the healthy and happy young girl she now was. The weight of her long imprisonment, her life under constant threat, had been lifted, and her pretty blue eyes showed the sparkle and interest of a child looking eagerly for tomorrow.

Although anxious to start back, Cooper had realized an immediate return trip down onto the flats might yet prove too much for him.

His wound had continued to heal without complication, but he was a wasted shadow of his former self. Clothes hung on his broad six-foot-plus frame like sailcloth from a mast, and his once unhurried, decisive step had dissolved into an ungainly shuffle. The ordeal, the weeks of short rations, shorter sleep, and loss of vitality from the wound in his back had extracted a heavy toll. The two days spent in Telluride, apart from the time spent purchasing the girl's new clothes and seeing to her other needs, he had spent resting in a hotel bed, rising only to take meals and short walks down the board sidewalks with Christie.

The girl's recuperative powers amazed him. The morning of their second day in town she had asked him eagerly when they might start for home. It suddenly occurred to him that home for her lay in a pile of weathered, dynamited kindling and the grave of an old man.

Where was he to take her? There was nothing left of Hap's cabin, and even if there was, he could not leave her there alone. Had she other relatives somewhere? Was he going to be forced to simply deposit her with Judge Bronson and let him place her into the fold of an orphanage or foster home? He shook his head, not liking that prospect overly much. Beyond that, she was nearly too old for that type of treatment: fifteen years old, reared in a land where women were often married at that age. No, for now, she needed to be brought into a home atmosphere with folks she knew and trusted.

He thought of Jane Porter. Her image in his mind was as sudden tender balm to a burn on his flesh. Her gentle eyes and smile beckoned him, called him home. Perhaps Jane could be persuaded to shelter the girl for a time, until something more permanent could be arranged.

And then, quite unbidden, another face — soft, dusky brown with large black eyes — forced its way into his thoughts; quiet, rain-soaked afternoons in a small adobe cabin, the sounds of her moving about in the kitchen, rocking gently before a crackling fireplace, the brush of full ripe lips on his own.

He had left them. He had ridden away from her and the boy. He had left in order to save his own life, and he had left them in peril of their own. Clara had assured Cooper they would be safe once he was away. But how did he know that to be true?

Cooper and the girl made camp in a tight stand of lodgepole pine, fairly sheltered from the drifts, a rock bank to their back to cut the force of the wind. While Cooper un-saddled, picketed, and grained the horses, Christie started a lively fire against the base of the rock bank. The lawman took note of the girl's woodcraft. Hap Hinkle had taught her well.

While Christie sorted out and began preparing their meal, Cooper lashed pine limbs together, forming a lean-to. He topped the structure with a canvas tarp, draped it down the sides to the ground, and secured it with stakes.

When finished, he threw their bedrolls inside and then moved off into the timber on foot to check their backtrail. Not that he feared being followed, but years of caution developed into patterns for life, and one careless oversight could as easily snatch that life away. Cooper made his share of mistakes — but carelessness was not one of them.

From a timbered game trail, he followed the road down over which they had just come. He was tired, but he slogged on for a half-mile and then crouched beneath an overhanging limb, rifle across his knees, and watched and waited.

It was dark when he returned to the camp. He noted again with approval how the girl, by her placement of the fire, had not only made an efficient blaze, but one that was concealed from the road, only a few hundred yards below them.

Her back was to him when he entered the

circle of light. At his step, she whirled, eyes wide with fear.

"I'm sorry, little lady. I should have called out. If you'd had a gun and shot me, you would have been within your rights."

Christie smiled, visibly shaken. "You were gone so long. I was worried something had happened to you."

He sank upon his bedroll in the opening of the lean-to. He was cold and the fire felt delicious, seeping slowly through his clothes, radiating warmth into his bones.

The girl handed him a cup of coffee.

"I used to make coffee for Hap all the time," she said. "I hope you like it." She smiled hopefully.

He tasted the coffee and was glad he didn't have to lie to her. "You take the cake. Set up a perfect camp and you make the best cup of coffee I've had in years." He might have been exaggerating a bit, but the glow in her eyes made it worth it.

She had kept their food warm on rocks near the fire, and now she handed him a plate. She seated herself with her own food on her bedroll and began eating, watching the lawman from the corner of her eye.

He said nothing but ate rapidly, almost ravenously, and when he finished he mopped the tin plate with a last morsel of a biscuit.

The fire sputtered and the girl jumped, startled. A shadow seemed to pass across her face.

After a silent, reflective moment, he said, "You'll probably never get what happened out of your mind altogether. But it'll fade. It will be easier to live with then." After another pause, he asked, hesitantly, "Did they —"

She shook her head. Without looking up, she answered, "Delwin — the one with the whip — wanted to, but Lance wouldn't allow it. All in all, Lance was pretty nice to me. When he got killed, I thought Delwin was going to get his way, but by then we were all near starvin', and I guess I wasn't lookin' so pretty no more 'cause he didn't bother me."

She set her plate aside and stood up, her slender form mantled by the fire's glow. "I'm glad they're dead, Marshal, even Lance, though he tried to help me a little bit. If they'd touched me — that way — I swear before heaven I'd've found a way to kill 'em myself."

For the next few days their course took them away from the wagon tracks; their progress was slowed, hampered by drifts, concealed deadfalls, and other hazards. At the end of the sixth day, they reached the flatlands.

All day long they had fought the glare of the sun on the unbroken snow. Finally, mid-afternoon, Cooper pulled his horse to a stop.

He untied his dark blue bandana from around his neck and, with his Bowie knife, punched two slits through the folded cloth. He gave the bandana to the girl, explaining that she was to wear it like a mask. The dark cloth around the eye holes would mute the glare enough to prevent snowblindness.

Next, he held a lighted match to his polished rifle barrel to produce soot, which he smeared thoroughly around and beneath his own eyes.

When he looked at her, Christie burst out laughing. "You look like a racoon!" she declared, her own eyes twinkling through the slits in the bandana mask.

"Gets the job done," Cooper said, smiling.

"What about the horses?" she asked. "Ain't you going to make them masks too?" She was still grinning.

"You just better hush," he warned, trying to appear serious. "The glare off that snow ain't no laughing matter."

They rode until nightfall, forded a small stream, and made camp amid a stand of willows. After they had eaten their dinner, Cooper brought out a can of peaches he had bought in Telluride. He pried open the can of the fruit with the tip of his knife and divided the contents.

Christie rolled her eyes in mock euphoria.

"I haven't had any canned peaches or canned nothin' in ages," she said between sloppy mouthfuls. "Hap, he was too tight to buy stuff like this. We always made do with the dried stuff. I would cook it up into pies. Hap, he loved them dried apple pies."

Cooper ate in silence, listening as she prattled on about her life with the old bandit.

"He was pretty good to you, wasn't he?" Cooper asked while the girl drained the last of the peaches direct from the can, juice running in streams on either side of her mouth.

"Hap was the best," she said, wiping her mouth on her shirtsleeve. "If there was anything I really needed, he would get it for me. Got me books, taught me to read. Got me Dulcie, my mare."

Her face clouded. "Dulcie was carryin' a foal too, when we got her. By an' by, she had her a little filly. Probably dead, unless someone came along an' tended her. When they took me off, they just left the little thing penned up. No feed. No water."

"Well," Cooper said offhandedly. "Maybe some kind soul came along and took care of her for you. Maybe some neighbor's looking after her."

Christie paused a moment, her eyes thoughtful. "We ain't got any close neighbors. None but Simms — old pack-rat codger lives off a ways. But he never did nothin' kind for nobody."

"Sometimes," said Cooper, pouring himself another cup of coffee and nudging with his toe a loose burning branch of mesquite deeper into the coals, "if you ask a person right, you can get them to do about anything."

She nodded, silent, picked up the end of a burning brand and began poking in the coals, eyes wide, lost in the flames.

After a time, she asked softly, "Marshal, what's going to become of me now?" Her voice betrayed no sadness, only a calm thoughtfulness.

"I've been giving that a thought or two myself."

"Hap's got a sister, in Denver. He was going to send me to school back there, an' have me live with her."

"That sounds like a fine idea. I could help you get in touch with her soon as we get back to Mexican Hat."

She hesitated. "Only trouble is, I ain't sure I want that now. It was different when Hap was alive. He wanted real bad for me to be a lady. An' I would've done it for him. But now I just got me to think about. I don't know if I'd be happy with that kind of life."

Cooper looked at her closely, saying nothing.

"I don't know," she faltered. "I think I belong here . . ." Her voice trailed off.

"Might be," offered Cooper, "you're a little bit scared? Starting a new life in a strange place is never easy."

She looked at him sharply, eyes flashing. "I ain't scared. I made it through all this, didn't I?"

"I don't mean that kind of scared," he quickly amended. "What I'm saying is sometimes we shortchange ourselves just because we don't want to face something new, something we don't understand right off."

He took a seat on the log beside her, cradling his coffee cup close. Steam from the cup rose into his whiskered face.

"Christie, just look at what you would have living in Denver. You would have an education, a whole lot of fine clothes, and good things. When the time's right, you would be meeting fine, upstanding young men — men with careers, not just getting by. One of them could take care of you better than any man you would meet out here."

"I don't need no one to take care of me," she answered. And then she grinned. "Not that I wasn't glad to see you show up when you did, Marshal."

He looked down into her young face, into eyes too blue, too wise. "You know what I'm saying, don't you, Christie?"

She nodded. "I think I'll have me a cup of coffee." She cast a quick, surreptitious glance at Cooper, half expecting him to object. When she was seated again, she said, "Hap only let me have coffee once in a while. But he taught me to make it real good. Don't you think it's good coffee, Marshal?"

Cooper looked at her and smiled gently. "Just think about it, will you?" he said. "No one is going to make you go there. But just don't throw away anything you might want later on."

She nodded soberly and sipped at her coffee, the flames from the fire dancing in her eyes.

CHAPTER 27

Two days later they camped in a thick grove of cottonwoods, barely fifty miles from Clara's cabin.

At the low elevation the snow was gone, but vast curtains of gray clouds hung over the land. The air was wet and still, and the crackle of the sage fire carried like muted gunfire. The noise made Cooper uneasy. Had he been alone, the camp would have been a cold one. But the girl was cold, and the mist hanging in the still air had dampened her hair and clothes, and she cuddled gratefully by the blaze.

"Sure is good to be out of the snow," she said, adding more sticks to the fire. "Maybe now I can get my feet dry."

"I wouldn't have the blaze too high," cautioned Cooper.

She looked at him closely. "We ain't seen no Indian sign. Least I ain't."

Cooper said no more, but that night he lay awake for a time. If they were to run into

Indians, namely Lame Badger and his crowd, it would be soon. Generally, only a dire absence of meat drove the Utes from their lodges in the dead of winter. But Lame Badger's band had been surviving off raids of farms, settlements, and foolhardy individuals. The chances of running into them now were great. And taking Christie into their midst did not set well with Cooper. But he knew he couldn't skirt the cabin and simply ride by, not without checking on the woman and the boy. The air had been heavy with danger when he had ridden away from them, and although in his condition at the time he could not have offered them much protection, he must now at least satisfy himself that they were safe.

For a time, he lay troubled, unable to sleep. At last he got up and banked Christie's bright fire so that it burned low, glowing amber against the night. Visitors might find their camp anyway, he reasoned. But that didn't mean they had to light the way for them.

Noon, two days later, they dropped down through a brush-choked cut and came out on the broad, flat area surrounding the small house.

The cabin stood silent and watchful. The white lace curtains had been sucked by the draft through the smashed-out windows and now hung lifeless, half in, half out, like the closed eyelids of a dead man. The sheep, knotted here and there, bleated mournfully and stood with hopeful heads up, awaiting the approaching riders.

Everything was havoc; furniture lay scattered upon the ground, dishes and clothing were tossed about, muddied and torn. A large chest of drawers lay on its side, standing rainwater puddled on its polished oak finish. Kerosene lamps, utensils, every household item the woman had owned seemed to be piled in the mud before the open door of the cabin.

Cooper dismounted in the midst of the sheep. One or two bolted. Most wandered about, bleating expectantly.

Christie started to dismount, but the lawman waved her back. "Let me have a look around first." If there was the possibility of death within the once-snug walls of the little house, Cooper did not think the girl needed to see any more of that.

He stepped onto the plank porch. Two sheep bolted through the front door, nearly knocking him over. He had started to draw his gun, but the fact the animals had taken refuge inside would preempt anyone laying in ambush within.

Nevertheless he entered cautiously, pausing every few feet to absorb in anger and frustration the total and wanton destruction of the woman's home.

They had done a thorough job, he thought bitterly, destroying, tearing apart, or smashing everything, every article the woman had assembled to make her home. Only a shell remained. Even the wooden bed frames had been smashed into kindling. Parts of the cast-iron stove had been scattered about, laying a black layer of soot across the devastation.

"My Lord!" whispered the girl, standing behind him in the doorway.

Cooper turned to her. "I told you to wait with the horses," he said, but she noticed he spoke without anger.

The girl walked about, picking up an odd piece of broken dish, a useless but at one time cherished item. "This is sad," she said softly. "Why would anyone want to do this?"

Cooper let out a frustrated sigh. "To show her in spades that she has nothing to come back for."

Christie placed the broken pieces on the window sill and wiped her sooty fingers on her pants.

"Did you know these folks, Marshal?"

"I knew them." He gazed about helplessly. "Indians trying to live in a white man's world."

The girl looked quickly about. "I don't see

no blood. Looks like it happened a while back, but still there'd be stains, wouldn't you think?"

"From the looks of it, I don't think they were hurt," Cooper agreed. "That bastard Lame Badger took them. He took her to wife and the boy as his son." He was silent a moment. "I shouldn't have left."

"You knew he was coming?" Christie asked.

"She knew he was coming. I didn't think he would go this far. I was wounded. She thought he would kill me." Cooper stopped abruptly. He was making excuses to the girl. A red flush crept up his neck and suffused his whiskered cheeks.

"You did the only sensible thing," she stated simply. "If you had stayed, you'd all been dead now. Not just you but them too."

He smiled weakly. "Do me a favor, will you? Take the horses down to the stock barn and see if you can find some feed for them. I'm going to look around and see if I can find enough food to get us through to town."

She had started toward the door, but stopped suddenly.

"Town?" she questioned. "We're going after 'em, ain't we?"

Cooper looked mildly amused. "No. *We* ain't going after 'em. *I'm* going after 'em. But first I'm taking you into town."

Christie's eyes flashed angrily. "What the hell kind of sense is that? You want to lose more time? They got at least three weeks start on ya right now."

"They're not going that far," the lawman answered, a bit irritated. "And quit that cussing. When we were talking one time, she mentioned about where Lame Badger's camp was. I think I can go right to it — or close enough anyways. It's on top of a landmark of sorts. But first I'm taking you into town."

By the hard look in her eyes, Cooper expected an angry reply. Instead, her face fell and she looked sad and a bit sullen.

"After what we been through?" she said in a hurt tone. "After all the time you spent savin' me, you'd just ride off an' leave me?"

"Look at it logically, Christie," Cooper tried patiently. "It'll be tough goin' all the way, and I'll have enough problems just looking after myself. You'd just be in the way."

Christie placed her hands on her hips. Her gaze was steady and issued a challenge.

"All right," she said flatly. "You want to talk logic — we'll talk logic. First off, to take me back to town will cost you three, maybe four, days. If you got any weather sense at all, you can see there's another storm on the way."

She paused, letting her voice sink in. Encouraged by Cooper's silence, she continued. "We can stay the night here and rest up and get a good early start in the morning." Her voice shifted to a wheedling tone. "I can really be a help, Marshal. I can track some. An' I can use a gun. You got an extra gun in your saddlebags. I saw it."

She read Cooper's helpless grin as one of capitulation. "You'll see," she continued hurriedly. "We'll get your friend an' her kid out of that mess in no time. An' we'll all be headin' back to town together."

Still smiling, Cooper placed a gentle hand on the girl's shoulder. "You must think I'm crazy, to think I'd even consider taking a child into the middle of a mess like that. First, I get you safe. Then I'll worry about the woman and the boy."

Christie's eyes sparked angrily. "That's stupid!" she cried, turning away sharply.

"Nevertheless," he answered firmly, "that's the way it is." And then a bit more gently, "You were right about one thing, though. We'll stay the night here and get a good rest. Now run along and tend the horses while I straighten things around."

Christie flounced through the door wordlessly, blond curls bobbing furiously beneath the brim of her hat.

Fifteen minutes later she returned, ashen-faced and trembling. Cooper had a fair start at clearing away some of the clutter and had started a fire in the cookstove, using bits of broken furniture. He looked up to find the girl staring blankly at him.

He laid aside a frying pan he had been scraping. "Are you all right?"

She nodded numbly. "There's two dead horses out there, in the pen. Coyotes been workin' at 'em, but I could see their throats been cut."

Cooper recalled the dray horses the boy had shown such care for. The animals had been the woman's and the boy's only transportation. That damn Indian had thought of everything, Cooper thought. It's a wonder he had not burned the house in the bargain.

"Did you get our horses put up?" he asked.

"There was a small shed on the other end away from the house. I found 'em some musty old hay, but it'll do to get 'em through." She looked about vacantly. "I can't believe anybody would do that to old horses," she said weakly.

"Oh, you think them Indians might play a little rougher than you thought, huh?" His tone was not sarcastic, but she reacted as though stung.

"I ain't a'scared of them, if that's what you mean," she answered stoutly. "And in case you hadn't thought about it, they could be plannin' on doin' to the woman and boy just what they did to them horses. Seems to be now you'd see the sense in us hurryin' after them."

Cooper looked at her, pained. They stood in the small kitchen next to the lean-to room where so very long ago, it seemed, he had convalesced. That room, too, had been painstakingly disassembled. The entire house seemed cold and alien, as though it had been vacant for years instead of days.

"Why don't you sweep up in the front room a bit," he said softly, turning back to the frying pan. "We'll need a place to throw our bedrolls. Maybe see if you can get a fire going in the fireplace. It's going to get cold tonight."

Cooper lay awake in his blanket, unable to sleep. His head was pillowed on his rolled-up coat. His eyes drifted about the room, illuminated by the flickering firelight. Thoughts of the house, the woman, the boy, danced in his restless mind like the jumping flames.

Cooper was not a man who spent a lot of time cross-examining his motives or exploring his reasons for doing anything; he simply did what was needed when it was needed. There was seldom time or need for reflection.

This was somehow different. His thoughts about the woman were a jungle of confused feelings. He was sharply drawn to her, to the tenderness she had shown him while nursing him back to health. He had had to admire her courage, her independence, and stoicism. And there was no lying about or getting away from the fact that he was drawn to her sensuality. She was an extremely attractive woman, and she carried herself with the full confidence that beauty warranted.

Compounding this confusion, Cooper felt the unpleasant, lingering weight of guilt. In Mexican Hat, Jane Porter waited. Though his commitment to Jane had not been a verbal one, nonetheless it was a solid, if tacit, understanding. Feigning ignorance of that understanding would be a lie Cooper would not, could not carry.

He rolled onto his side, pulled the blanket about his ears, and listened to the night sounds. The rain had begun and it dripped from the eaves. Cooper had found some boards and had nailed them across the broken-out windows. With the fire in the fireplace, it was quite comfortable within the snug cabin.

The lawman was desperately tired. And his back, though well along toward healing, had begun hurting him early in the evening. He frowned in the darkness. What he needed was whiskey. He could almost feel the spidery warmth hit his stomach, explode and creep out to the aching joints, relax the taut muscles and bring on the sleep he so badly longed for.

He looked across the fireplace at the small bundle that was Christie, snuggled deep into her blankets, lost in the innocent sleep of the very young. How beautiful she is, Cooper thought, the firelight dancing from each golden curl, touching and blushing the clear, calm face.

She had won. He would take her with him because she had been right — time was the important factor now. The longer he waited to attempt a rescue of the woman and the boy, the less likely his chance of success.

He hated the prospect of taking Christie from one form of danger only to thrust her within the grasp of another threat.

In the morning, Christie put together a filling breakfast of hotcakes and the last of their sidemeat. Despite the overcast sky and the oppressive weight of the days ahead, the hot coffee and the breakfast, along with Christie's ebullient spirits, seemed to make Cooper's morning almost all right.

The girl was in a chattering mood. He had not said so, but she somehow knew she had won; she would accompany Cooper after the woman and the boy. If she was at all apprehensive about the danger element, it was not showing. She moved about the house like a bird, packing their limited food supply, rolling up bedding.

When everything was in readiness, Cooper saddled the horses and brought them to the front door. The packhorse was loaded, then Cooper and the girl mounted and sat looking at the sad little rain-soaked structure.

"She had a very nice home here," observed Christie solemnly. "Maybe if all this works out, we can stick around a while an' help them fix the place up a bit."

Cooper gave her a thoughtful glance and pulled the steeldust's head around. He started the steeldust north, the girl following in his tracks, leading the packhorse behind her paint mare. The drizzle turned into a light but steady rain.

CHAPTER 28

A single Ute warrior guided his horse along the ridge, the animal responding to mere touches from the Indian's moccasined toes. He was a youthful warrior, and he rode with head erect, black hair flowing unencumbered to his shoulders. He was dressed in winter buckskins. A vest made from furry wolf skins covered his deep chest. Across the pommel of his Indian-made saddle he held an old Winchester in his brown hands.

He rode the horse on a course paralleling that of the riders of the flatlands far below. His eyes followed intently the progress of the big white man and the girl.

It was cold. A pale, washed-out sun battled against the leaden sky, and a strong breeze blew from the southwest, ruffling the horse's mane and the gray wolf hair on the warrior's vest. An older warrior would have been entertaining thoughts of his warm lodge and the comfort his squaw would afford him on a day such as this, but the warmth in the belly of the young Ute came from the fire of eagerness, a desire to win the praise and recognition of Lame Badger. For this one was new to the growing band of warriors leaving the old men and following after the wrathful, charismatic war chief. To be singled out for a mere word of praise by Lame Badger was worth more than the accolades of all the old men. For Lame Badger was doing things. He was raising up from the corpse of a dead tribe a new brand of warrior, one that killed the white man and took the white man's possessions, his cattle, his guns, and his women: a warrior that returned evil for evil.

The big white man below, riding bundled against the wind, would die, either today or tomorrow, and the young warrior would be commended for his alertness.

The Indian's first impulse was to determine the direction in which the man and the girl traveled, then to ride to camp and report and perhaps lead the warriors to an interception point. But now, as he rode unmindful of the cold, he formed a new plan. What would his chief bestow upon him were he to ride into camp with the girl in tow and the big white man stretched cold across his own saddle?

Also, the horse the white man rode, though appearing worn-out, was a big, fine one. By custom it would belong to the warrior who

238

killed the white man. The youth was unsure about the girl; he supposed he would have first claim to her also. But with his new young wife waiting in his lodge, one more woman might tax his physical stamina, and his tolerance.

The warrior spent a sleepless, freezing night hidden among the rocks within a quarter mile of the glow of the white man's campfire. He lay on a small crest, his pony tethered to a sage pile in the draw behind him.

Once, when the big man walked out to his horses, the warrior was almost certain the man was aware of his presence. It seemed once that the white man had looked directly at his place of concealment. No matter. The man and the girl would sleep, the warrior would not. And at first light, when sleep was heaviest upon them, he would make his move. He would kill the man, and take his body and the girl to Lame Badger.

He settled down to wait with all the resolve of a man waiting for his destiny to unfold.

The hours dragged on, and the night grew long; he was tired and very, very cold. He felt his eyes grow heavy, his resolve weaken.

His head snapped up. He had been dozing, face buried in the gray wolf nap of his vest. His head and shoulders were covered with a layer of fine, gritty ice. A violent shudder shook his cramped frame.

It was still dark, but in the eastern sky a perceptible glow filtered through the crystal air, through the falling tiny particles of ice.

He roused himself, rubbing his eyes with numb fingers, and raised himself up to a point where he could view the camp.

Below, all was still. It was a good time to move. He must work his way closer into camp, before they awakened.

He would kill the man first. The girl was of no consequence. Once the white man fell, it was likely the female would revert to form and simply stand there, screaming hysterically.

The first rifle shot must count. The young warrior had seen the way the big white man moved. He was a man to be respected. He was wary; his manner alert. A shadow passed over the young warrior's spirit and he shivered. This time it was not from the cold.

Christie's eyes fluttered open. Something had awakened her. She lay still, listening, breathing through her mouth.

From the shelter of their windbreak, she heard the horses stamp and blow restlessly.

Her feet were cold. She raised up on one elbow and looked out the opening of the shelter. The fire had, of course, long since burned itself out. A few smoldering ends of sage branches remained.

She yawned, threw back the blankets, and pulled on her boots. It was cold — a bone-aching cold — and she was shaking when she slipped into Cooper's heavy, fleece-lined coat. Her own was rolled into a pillow beneath the marshal's head. She pulled her wool stocking cap down over her curls and slipped out of the shelter to build up the fire and put the coffee on.

Christie was not prone to pampering herself. With few exceptions she had risen every morning before Cooper, freshened up quickly, and started breakfast. Usually the coffee had boiled before Cooper even rolled out of bed.

For the lawman it was a luxury, and he basked in it. Though often awake, he was given to lying abed in a leisurely manner until he smelled the aroma of fresh coffee. It was a good feeling. Cooper found he truly enjoyed the girl's company. She was a complex, unfathomable individual, but she was also polite and thoughtful. She had assumed the role of camp cook completely on her own.

As he lay in the warmth of his bedroll, listening to her stir about, a shot rang out.

Christie pitched forward. She spun about and landed on her back in the smoldering ruins of the fire. She let out a low cry and struggled to sit upright.

Another shot smacked the frozen air. This one passed harmlessly overhead. It struck somewhere near the picketed horses. The animals jerked at their tethers and snorted.

Christie managed to sit up. A bright red stain soaked through the shoulder of Cooper's coat. The girl's backside was covered with ashes and clinging live coals.

Before the report of the second shot had died away, Cooper was at her side, kneeling in the snow in his stocking feet, six-gun in hand.

The lawman passed one arm about the girl's middle, lifted her from the ground, and nearly threw her beneath the tarp cover. The boulders skirting the makeshift tent would ward off any stray bullets.

But Cooper had no intention of letting himself be penned down in the tent. He meant to take the fight to the bastard's doorstep.

He glanced down at the girl. She lay in a crumpled heap, unconscious, tousled hair spilled over her white, pinched face.

He thrust his six-gun into his waistband and quickly covered her with a blanket. Drawing on his boots, he picked up his Winchester and slipped from beneath the tarp.

The falling ice particles pecked at the brim

of his hat as his eyes searched the whitened landscape. He took particular note of the dark areas beneath the clumps of mesquite and the boulders large enough to shield a man's body.

After a few minutes he detected a movement, not much, the bare twitching of a mesquite branch.

He levered a shell into the chamber and fired a quick shot into the area beneath the growth. The limb jumped, a dark form flitted from the bush to a nearby cluster of boulders.

That was enough. Cooper slipped up through the gaps between the boulders, crouched low, working his way rapidly up the slight rise behind the shelter. The whisper of the falling ice particles helped to muffle his efforts. He realized this would serve equal purpose for the attacker.

He removed his spurs and moved on silent cat feet, working his way between the boulders. Behind him a horse nickered. He moved invisibly through the storm, some distance from camp, Winchester at the ready.

Ahead, and to one side, a horse coughed. There was a brushing sound, as of leather against stone, and then only the steady whisper of the frozen crystals on the surface of snow.

And then he was suddenly there, charging his horse directly at the lawman. Cooper had a glimpse of a triumphant smile etched on the young Indian's face. And then the smile was frozen in eternity as the bullet fired from Cooper's Winchester crashed through the forehead and entered the brain.

The running horse veered sideways, brushing Cooper's shoulder as it passed. And the warrior, still clutching his rifle, pitched into the snow at the lawman's feet.

CHAPTER 29

The Anvil. It was merely a butte, sealed off on three sides by sharp, windswept shoulders, five hundred feet high. One end was undercut, like the flat end of an anvil; hence the name. The only access to the top, on the north, west, and south sides, was by a series of narrow goat trails, easily defended. On the east side the butte tapered into a long, flat area, gradually rising into a thick matting of scrub pine and then on into the slopes above. Underground springs, fed by runoff from the slopes, afforded a plentiful water supply even in the driest weather. And there was grass for horses and areas for planting corn to eat and for forage.

It was virtually impregnable. A handful of fighting men above could hold off the advance of a thousand men from below. If the long knives could somehow attain the top, they would find Lame Badger's band had disappeared into the pines.

Cooper paid grudging respect to the sagacity

of Lame Badger in choosing the mountain for his retreat.

He rode with the girl cradled on the saddle before him. Behind rode the young Ute warrior, lashed with ropes to his pony's back. Following, lead ropes tied to the tails of the horse ahead, came Christie's mare and the packhorse.

The girl was unconscious. It had taken Cooper much too long to staunch the flow of blood from her shoulder. Though the bullet had passed through, she lay waxen-faced and limp in his arms.

The sleet had quit for the time, but the clouds still hung gray and heavy and threatening.

He pulled up at the base of the citadel, giving the horses a blow and himself a chance to scan the upper rim of the rock. He fancied he saw faint tendrils of smoke, but against the murky sky, he could not be sure. There was no doubt in his mind that he was being watched. He guessed he knew now how a mouse felt under the scrutiny of a hawk.

Cooper started on. A sharp downdraft brought the smell of woodsmoke and the wet, cold flavor of the increasing snow.

Despite the cold, Cooper was sweating. And it was not just the perilous trip up the side of the mountain that had him worried. His own mortality, and the life of the girl, weighed heavy upon him.

He was riding upward into a near-hopeless situation. Were the girl to survive, she would most surely be taken into the tribe and married off to the first buck with enough goods to tempt Lame Badger. Or the guerilla chief himself might take the girl into his lodge, a second — or third — wife beside Clara.

Cooper's life was surely forfeit. He had killed too many of them, first, in the attack in the valley and now this young warrior, barely out of puberty. The best he could hope for would be a quick bullet to the brain, a painless knife thrust to the throat.

The narrow trail squirmed this way and that, working its way to the butte's rim, five hundred feet above the desert floor.

Cooper's visibility was all but wiped out by the swirling, stinging flakes of snow. It was just as well, he figured. Looking over the side of that precipitous drop would only unnerve him further, and already he could feel his shirt sweat-glued to his back.

Every few minutes he reined in, giving the ragged and weary horses a rest. He had small worry now about the animals spooking and charging over the edge. They were too far gone to do anything but stand and tremble with the strain of the climb.

The smell of woodsmoke grew stronger and Cooper began to sense a delicate tickle along his spine. The ears of the steeldust picked up and stood forward, twitching.

The lawman glanced down at the unconscious girl in his arms. "One way or another you're going to get your help now, little gal," he promised. He placed a hand on her brow. The fever was worsening. He had neither time nor material to tend properly to the girl's wound. Staunching the flow of blood with a strip of cloth from his shirttail had been the best he could manage. With her condition as such, the decision to make immediately for the Indian camp was the only one possible. There would be food and shelter there, if not herbs to heal her wound.

There was no point in trying to hide the death of the young Indian. Cooper's only hope was that Lame Badger might possess a sense of fair play and realize that the youth's attack had been unprovoked and that his killing had been totally in self-defense. That the lawman had brought the body home should account for something. But then you could never count on the Indian mind. What seemed right and proper to a white man might be mortal sin in an Indian's estimation. Notwithstanding, the girl needed help beyond that which Cooper could provide out in the open, windswept plain. He had to chance it.

They appeared like spirits out of the swirling snow, astride horses crested with white, their own shoulders and black hair matted with ice. Six Indians stood in shadowy silence as Cooper crested the rim and pulled his sad little caravan out onto the Anvil's top. Even had it been a fighting situation, he would have had no chance, for they were about him in a flash. Wisely he checked his first reaction and kept his hands clear of his guns. He gathered Christie's limp, feverish form to him and returned the glittering stare of the Indian closest to him.

The older Indian, standing his pony stolidly before Cooper, asked, "You killed him?"

"After he shot the girl and tried to kill me. I do not believe the Utes to be killers of young girls. I must believe he thought it was me he was shooting at. The girl was wearing my coat."

The older Indian seemed to consider this while the younger warriors charged their ponies around, churning the ground to slush.

Cooper ignored them, his eyes locked upon those of the older warrior.

Several moments passed. At last the Ute said, "You must have another reason for climbing our mountain, other than to die."

"I need help for the girl," Cooper replied. "And I brought your dead back to you."

"You think," said the Ute, "that by bringing back the body of our dead we would forget the one who killed him?"

"I ask you to forget nothing. I ask only for help for the girl."

At that moment Christie stirred and moaned softly. Her eyes fluttered open, and she looked up uncertainly into Cooper's haggard face.

"She is yours?" asked the Indian.

Cooper nodded. There was no point in a long and involved explanation.

The older Indian raised his hand, and the warriors ceased their howling and pulled their horses to a halt. They stood quietly, hard eyes fixed on Cooper.

"We will do what we can for the girl," the warrior said. "Lame Badger will decide what is to become of you."

He wheeled his horse and motioned for Cooper to follow. After a few steps he paused.

"I thank you for bringing my son home," he said simply. "I will do what I can to help you live the day through."

After the unconscious girl was taken from him and given over to the care of the women, Cooper was jerked roughly from the saddle, his weapons taken, and his arms bound securely behind his back with narrow thongs of rawhide.

For a time the young warriors amused themselves by buffeting the lawman about. They formed a circle, pushing him about, jostling him, trying to make him fall. When finally he did, they refused to let him rise again. Each time he reached his knees they knocked him back into the snow.

One of the young men danced forward, parodying a charging buffalo with fingers pointing from his head like horns. He struck Cooper in the face, then danced back to the howls of laughter from his comrades. On the heels of that success he started forward again, only to be brought up short by a sharp command from the old warrior whose son Cooper had killed.

"Lame Badger will see you," the Indian whispered up close, helping Cooper to his feet and leading him by one bound elbow from the circle of Indians. "I will speak on your behalf, but the final word will be his."

Cooper looked at the Indian. "I thank you for that. Worse comes to worse, I'd appreciate it if you would look after the girl."

"She will not be harmed. In spite of what my son did, we do not make war on children."

Cooper was led to a snow-covered skin lodge. The warrior pulled aside the hide flap covering the doorway and motioned him to enter. So low was the opening, Cooper was compelled to bend double to enter.

The flap dropped behind him and he stood a moment, his eyes growing accustomed to the dim light, waiting for what was to come next.

The interior was close with smoke and cooking smells. Besides the hazy flames from the sage fire, the only light filtered down from the narrow smoke hole at the top of the conical structure. It was surprisingly warm within.

Lame Badger was reclining on a deer hide pallet, propped up on one elbow. It was a moment before Cooper's eyes adjusted to where he could make out the man's features.

When their eyes met, the Indian motioned to the lawman to sit. Arms bound behind him, it was a difficult maneuver. When it was accomplished Cooper waited for the Indian to speak first.

"I'm curious," said Lame Badger. "I expected you to come after the woman. If you returned to the house and found her gone, you would know that I had her. But why," he asked, "did you bring the girl? She could only hinder your attempt to retrieve the woman and the boy, no matter how stupid or useless such an effort might be."

"The girl wasn't part of the plan," Cooper

admitted. "It just worked out that way. If you're around her long enough, you'll find out she doesn't take no for an answer very often."

Lame Badger smiled. "She'll learn very quickly to take no for an answer. Or any other answer I choose to give her."

Cooper's arms had begun to ache. The leather thongs were very tight. Despite the warmth in the hut, his feet were cold and he was hungry.

"Right now," the lawman said evenly, "we are at your mercy. You can kill me anytime. But I brought the girl here because one of your young men shot her. If you're the man I think you are, you'll help her."

"She is being cared for," Lame Badger replied carelessly. "If she lives she will become one of us. One day she will marry one of our warriors. Or perhaps I will take her as a wife. Her future is uncertain, but yours is not. You will die. Today, tomorrow —" He shrugged.

"You wouldn't want to give me my guns and a fighting chance, would you? I guarantee you'll get your money's worth of excitement."

The Indian did not answer. He rose to his feet and pushed the hide flap aside.

Two warriors, snow clinging to their shoulders, entered the hut, pulled Cooper to his feet, and led him out into the storm.

At the doorflap, Cooper jerked free and called over his shoulder. "I want to see Clara, Lame Badger. And the boy. Coming all this way, I think I've earned that much."

Lame Badger, framed in the opening with large, moist flakes clinging to his hair and brows, glared at the white man. "You've earned nothing but your own death." He gestured sharply. Rough hands seized Cooper by his bound arms and he was led away through the swirling snow.

Cooper awoke, stiff with cold. His guard was gone, his blanket empty. The fire in the center of the lodge had gone out, only blackened embers remained.

The lawman had struggled for hours with his bonds, scraping raw the skin about his wrists. He had nearly worked one arm free before exhaustion had claimed him. Even if he were free he didn't know what he could accomplish besides hastening his own death. Escape without the girl was out of the question. He simply would not leave her to the future Lame Badger had outlined for her. And in her present condition, to move her would be to kill her.

Lying on his side he renewed his efforts on the leather thongs binding his arms. After a few minutes he had gained enough slack to pull one arm free.

He sat up and was unwrapping the thongs from the other wrist when the flap was pulled aside and Clara stepped into the dim lodge.

"You needn't have bothered," she said, using her knife to cut the thongs. "I was told I may release you now anyway."

Cooper grinned sadly. "You mean I worked all night for nothing?"

She sat down next to him on his sleeping mat. "You made this entire trip for nothing." She paused, "Why *did* you come?"

Cooper shrugged. "I found your house all torn up. I had some grand notion of riding in here and pulling you and the boy out. Things got complicated when that buck shot Christie." He sighed and shook his head. "Well, hell, I just couldn't ride on, not knowing what had become of you."

"Now you know."

"How is the girl doing? Have you seen her?"

"She will live," answered the woman. "She needs food and much meat, to build her up. She lost much blood. She awoke once to ask about you."

"Will they let me see her?" His tone was cautious. There was something different, something strange in Clara's manner. She was as lovely as ever, and his mind was drawn, almost against his will, to the kiss she had placed on his lips the afternoon he had ridden away from her cabin. In that sweet moment she had been warm to him, available. The warmth was gone. Left was great caution, born of — what? Fear for her life, or the life of her child? Maybe a fear for Cooper's life?

She answered him almost sharply. "Whether or not they let you see her depends on Lame Badger."

"Has he hurt you?" Cooper asked, rubbing circulation back into his arms.

"Not in the way you are thinking. He wants me willing, and he is prepared to wait. He has hit me," she added simply, "but that means nothing. That is the Ute way."

"And how long is he going to wait for you to have a change of heart?"

She was slow in answering. "He will not have to wait much longer. Now that you and the girl are here."

She rose quickly to her feet, giving him no time to question her further. She slipped beneath the doorflap and was gone.

CHAPTER 30

Cooper threw his large frame on the pallet of evil-smelling skins, laced his fingers behind his neck, and stared up at the woven sticks of his roof. He needed to do some tall thinking.

He wondered about the steeldust and the girl's paint mare. The ponies of the Utes were in good condition. It would be a safe guess the prisoners's horses were being adequately cared for as well.

As he lay, pondering thought after discouraging thought, his eyes closed and he fell asleep in the chill hut. His hat covered his eyes, his arms were folded across his chest, hugging stoutly to his own body warmth.

They would kill him. Of that Cooper was certain. He felt fear, but no panic. He had no wish to die, but he knew life offered no guarantees. He regretted most the girl. It was unlikely they would kill her, but the life awaiting her among the Utes was a poor alternative. Still, she would be alive. And life meant hope.

Cooper cursed. There was little he could do about the circumstances, but he had to try something. They couldn't kill him any more dead standing on his feet, fighting, than lying helpless under a dirty blanket in a lice-infested hut.

He had no weapon other than his fists. And he was weak and sore. But a stout determination began building up inside him. No longer would he be a helpless victim. If they were going to kill him, he meant to sell his life dearly. The fire of his will burned strong. His sore muscles grew taut and battle-ready as he went to the doorflap.

He lifted the flap carefully. It was a gray, murky dawn with large flakes of snow falling from a leaden sky.

He glanced quickly about. There seemed to be some activity in the camp, unusual considering the early hour. A small knot of warriors was clustered around the central hut. As memory served him, from his one interview with Lame Badger, this was the leader's hut.

A plan was forming, a desperate, foolhardy effort. So hopeless were its chances of success that its only virtue lay in that it was the only plan that came to mind.

He pushed aside the doorflap and stepped from the hut. A shudder passed through his frame, and he wondered which Indian now wore his warm, fleece-lined coat.

Keeping low, Cooper slipped behind hut after hut, working his way toward the cluster of mounted warriors. As he moved, he glanced continually about, anxious that he not be seen and an early warning be sounded. He would have one chance. Failure would mean instant death, although, viewed in that light, Cooper felt he had little to lose. To lay about and do nothing was to simply await his execution.

It was cold and the new snow squeaked beneath his boots, so he stepped carefully, walking in the unbroken, pillowy snow where possible.

Somehow he reached the back side of Lame Badger's lodge and knelt close up to the structure, trying to quiet his ragged breathing and thumping heart. The exertion of staggering silently through the snow had taxed his already bone-weary frame. A man's body was not meant to be treated this way, he concluded with a wry and insane smile.

When his breathing had returned to nearly normal, he began an inspection of the outside back wall of Lame Badger's lodge: buffalo and deer hides over a wattle frame, sealed at the bottom and about a foot up the wall with a mixture of mud and manure. In several places cracks had appeared in the foundation, running vertically down from the top, disappearing under the snow.

Cooper thrust his hands into the snow, regretting instantly the loss of his gloves. He dug the snow away from the foundation, clearing a two-foot section, and found, as expected, that the mud had softened from contact with the wet snow.

He dug slowly into the foundation, taking great care that no sound be made to give away his presence. The slight digging noise he made grappling with the sodden chunks was muffled, he hoped, by the falling snow.

Periodically he paused to listen to the conversation in course on the far side of the hut. There seemed much concern over a band of deer that had wandered conveniently close to the base of the Anvil. Lame Badger's men contended this must be some remote herd that had wandered by, since the surrounding desert area had been well hunted during their long stay.

Cooper smiled as he worked. Lame Badger's gutteral responses to his warriors' questions and comments sounded impatient and peevish.

Cooper gasped as one fingernail tore loose against a shard of rock implanted in the mud foundation. But he persisted, and a moment later felt his hand penetrate through the wall into the hut's warm interior. Another few minutes and he had cleared a hole large enough to allow him to pass through.

One more quick glance about, and he turned and launched himself into the dark opening.

He went in fast. Because Lame Badger stood outside talking with his warriors did not mean the hut was empty.

The skin doorflap was partly askew, permitting enough light for him to see Clara.

She started to rise, although no alarm showed in her eyes.

He placed a warning finger to his lips.

"I suspected it might be you," she whispered calmly. "We have no dogs left in camp large enough to tear a hole that quickly. The larger dogs have all been eaten." There was in her tone a touch of humor. And then she added more soberly, "You really should not do this. You are not well, and you will accomplish nothing."

"Better than lying there waiting for Lame Badger to stamp my ticket. If I'm going to die, I guess I might as well pick the where and how."

He had moved to the doorflap and now crouched by the opening, listening. The conversation seemed to be resolved. Lame Badger should be entering the hut in seconds.

Cooper glanced quickly about. It was then

he saw the boy's two large black eyes regarding him from the far side of the hut, curious, questioning, utterly fearless.

Before either could speak, the doorflap was jerked aside as Lame Badger stooped and entered the hut.

There was no time for a decision or reflection on the best method. Cooper, from his kneeling position beside the door, slammed a fist into Lame Badger's stomach, dropping the Indian to his knees in shock, gasping for air.

Cooper seized Lame Badger's left arm, twisting it behind him, forcing the hand up between his shoulder blades. At the same time he circled the thick neck with his own left arm, effectively controlling the flow of air to the lungs.

Whatever the woman and the boy had expected of Cooper, this was not it. The woman stared, hand clasped over her mouth. The boy screamed a warning in Ute, a cry for help. He threw his small body at Cooper, kicking and striking at the defenseless lawman, while Cooper, intent on holding the large Indian in check, could do nothing but try to shrug off his young tormenter.

Outside the hut, Lame Badger's departing warriors heard the boy's cries, wheeled their horses, and raced back. A half-dozen strong, they all tried to crowd through the small hut opening at the same moment.

When one finally managed to push his way through, the sight that greeted him was his chief, held helpless, and apparently in his death throes, by the lawman.

Cooper stood against the far wall, using Lame Badger's body as a shield. He maintained a hammerlock on the Indian's left arm. Across Lame Badger's throat he had lain the Indian's own sheath knife.

Two of the warriors crowded into the hut. A third stood with his head and shoulders thrust through the door.

Cooper, finally, with an impatient sweep of his arm, sent the boy rolling headlong into his mother. She clasped him, and the boy, from behind her restraining arms, glared at the marshal.

"No one needs to get hurt," Cooper said.

The warriors were armed with old rifles. One was shoved menacingly into the marshal's face.

"Kill him!" ordered Lame Badger in a strangled whisper. The warrior's finger was frozen on the trigger. The purposeful look in Cooper's eyes left no doubt of his intent.

The warrior looked at his leader. Beneath the mask of hatred there was fear. Lame Badger knew that his life now hung by a thread.

"Sure, you can kill me," Cooper said calmly, almost gently, "but I'll take half his windpipe with me as I fall."

The big Indian struggled under the pressure of the blade. As if to emphasize his point Cooper moved slightly the hand holding the knife. Droplets of blood appeared from under the knife edge and trickled down the throat onto the brown chest.

"Just stand easy," Cooper said to Lame Badger, planting his own feet a bit more solidly. "If we use our heads, both of us might come out of this alive."

Lame Badger's eyes flashed a warning to the two Indians in the doorway. He felt the knife blade ease off against his throat.

"What do you want?" Lame Badger demanded.

"What the hell do you think I want?"

Lame Badger's left arm had lost feeling. The shoulder, with arm twisted behind, was in excruciating agony. He moved slightly, pulling forward to ease the pressure.

Cooper jerked the arm higher and felt the Indian rise on his toes.

"Well," Cooper said, sustaining the pressure. "I'm waiting."

The Ute nodded. He spoke through clenched jaws. "You will be allowed to leave."

"Not good enough. Me and the girl, and

the woman and her son. We all go."

"Never!" Lame Badger hissed. "If we both die, then let it be so!" To the warriors he said, "Take him!"

Clara leaped to her feet. "No! No one dies!" She flung herself between Lame Badger and the warriors' rifles. "Listen to me." She turned pleading eyes first on Lame Badger and then on Cooper. "No one dies," she repeated in a whisper.

Sudden anger welled inside Cooper's chest. He was tired, he was sick, and his patience was gone.

"If you can talk sense to him, go ahead," he snapped at the woman. "I've had it with this sonofabitch. I'm as ready to die as he is. And I ain't leavin' here without you and the girl."

The woman nodded, eyes wide. She turned to Lame Badger. "Remember," she said breathlessly, "when we talked. I agree now, to everything you asked. But you must let Cooper and the girl go."

"No!" Cooper bellowed, all but jerking Lame Badger off the ground. "We all go or none!"

The woman turned on him savagely. "Ride out now. Take the girl and leave. If not for yourself, then for her."

"And what about you? Why are you so damn willing to stay all of a sudden?"

Her chin was out, firm. "I'm willing. That is enough." She turned to Lame Badger. "Do you agree?"

Sweat poured off the Indian's face. He was in a great deal of pain. Cooper, in his last enthusiastic effort, had very nearly dislocated the Indian's shoulder.

He hesitated a moment and then nodded. "Cooper goes . . . ," he said slowly between clenched teeth, "and the girl." He looked challengingly into the woman's eyes. "You and the boy stay."

Cooper maintained his hold on the Indian. "Well, I guess now that the two of you have come to an agreement I'm supposed to follow suit."

"Turn him loose," she said, imploring him with large, black eyes.

The knife trembled in Cooper's hand. His jaws were clenched in an exhausted, spent fury.

"I haven't agreed to nothing yet," he muttered, again pressing the blade against the taut, brown skin. "We all ride out or nothing." He jerked up savagely on the Indian's arm. A low cry escaped Lame Badger's lips, and his knees started to buckle. Simultaneously, the two warriors made as if to move forward.

"Let him go, Cooper," she ordered. "It's my choice. I want to stay with him."

The knife relaxed a bit. Lame Badger's arm was lowered an inch closer to his belt, and the big Ute actually sighed with relief.

"What about the boy?" said Cooper. "You thinking of him?"

"This is where he belongs. I can see that now. He never wanted the white man's world. He's always been Ute. He's always felt as a Ute."

The knife dropped from Cooper's hand. He released Lame Badger's arm and took a step toward the woman.

"I could change the boy's mind," he said to her, "if I had the chance."

She shook her head. "There is no need to change anyone's mind. This is where we belong — with him."

"His world is dead. He'll be killed in a fight or the army will hang him. The rest of his group — those still alive — will be stuck on the reservation. And you'll be stuck there with them."

She dropped her eyes. "It is what I want . . ."

The two warriors moved swiftly, taking Cooper by the arms. The third Indian squeezed through the doorway and advanced on the lawman, rifle butt upraised.

Lame Badger raised an arm, the one that still worked, and waved them away.

"My word is given," he muttered, looking at Cooper with eyes filled with hate. "No harm is to come to him or the girl."

Cooper ignored the Indians behind him, unconscious and uncaring of his helplessness, or their threat. All his attention was centered upon the woman.

"You are doing this to save our lives —"

"Stop it!" she exploded. "Go back where you belong, for God's sake. Go *now*."

He stared helplessly, first at the woman and then the boy.

Finally his wide shoulders sagged. He stumbled weakly to one side and caught himself with an arm against the hut wall.

"Well, I guess that's that." He started for the door, brushing aside the Indians as though they were mere shadows, and continued through the Utes clustered outside.

No one raised a hand to him, moving aside to let him pass like the prow of a ship slicing through the waves.

The snow had stopped, but it was growing colder. Cooper shivered. He again wondered vaguely, disinterestedly, what had become of his coat. The chill bit through the sleeves of his flannel shirt. His resistance to the cold was gone. He let it saturate him, seep into his bones.

When he reached his hut he was shivering uncontrollably.

The days passed. Cooper's cuts and bruises began to fade and with the regular meals prepared by one of the old women, his strength began to return.

Christie, in like manner, was improving rapidly. Through the use of some remedy known to the Utes, the infection had been arrested, the wan, pinched look left her cheeks, and she began to flourish like a spring flower.

Together they took short walks around the camp, sometimes walking to the edge of the precipice and viewing on clear days the vast, white winter wasteland running west to the horizon.

Cooper delighted in the air, the clarity, and the heady freshness that he could feel all the way down to his toes. He found the walks always a welcome relief from the cramped mustiness of the hut.

His guns had been returned to him. He had gone to Lame Badger and demanded them, and also his coat, which he had spotted on the back of a meaty warrior. Though smelling evil of grease and woodsmoke and unwashed Indian, he welcomed its fleece-lined warmth.

Daily they saw to their horses. Lame Badger had planned his headquarters well, provisioning a fenced-off area with corn stalks and fodder, and the steeldust and Christie's paint mare basked in a new layer of fat.

The girl was sleeping in Cooper's hut now. Across their fire that night she noted the troubled knit to his brow.

"I managed to steal some more of our supplies back today," she said brightly. "We got enough to make it back to town in fine shape. How about we leave tomorrow?"

Cooper looked up, surprised and, she thought, pleased.

"You sure you're up to it? We'll be on the trail three, four, maybe five days, depending on the weather."

"I can handle it," she answered, not without a note of pride. "If I have to I'll help hold you in the saddle."

Cooper laughed, and the sound in the dismal hut lifted Christie's spirits soaring. They were going to be all right now. She just knew it.

Cooper saw Clara rarely, and when he did he made an effort to move immediately and as unobtrusively as possible from the area. He did not want to speak to her. He did not want to look at her. The sooner he could put miles between himself and her, the better he would feel. Of that he was certain.

On one occasion, when he and Christie were returning from a walk around the perimeter of the camp, they came unexpectedly upon the woman. She and the boy were engaged in packing clean snow into a melting pot.

There was one strained look between them before Cooper averted his eyes, clasped Christie's hand tightly, and continued on. The woman's mouth opened as though to speak, but then she too turned away.

CHAPTER 31

They left the camp at first light. The previous night everything had been gathered together so that it was a simple matter of loading up the packhorse, saddling up, and riding out.

Early though it was, the breakfast fires had been kindled and a few brave souls were stomping about the snow, doing morning chores. The ever-present sentries, watching through the cold night along the icy cliff edge, had been replaced and had themselves returned to camp to crawl into their blankets.

There was no one to whom they should say their farewells. Those Indians up and about seemed to take no notice of their departure. And that was just as Cooper wished it. Cold miles passing under his saddle would help smother the resentment and hurt in his heart.

The icy trail down the cliff face had been chewed up enough by the coming and going of the wood gatherers to where it was not so hazardous as when he had ascended.

Cooper took it good and slow, marking each

turn carefully, dismounting and leading the stock over the troublesome areas.

Christie, swathed in warm blankets from her head to below her knees, chatted incessantly. Cooper listened, making one-word responses when necessary, otherwise letting the girl prattle on. It was plain her intent: she hoped to distract him, take his mind off his hurt. She would never know how miserably her efforts were failing. In light of her obvious concern for him, Cooper's fondness for the girl grew.

The greasewood fire had been laid amid the cluster of large boulders, and the heat was reflected in such a way that quite soon a fair measure of comfort was felt. The girl, once the first chill had been driven from her bones, set about putting together their simple evening meal. Cooper busied himself with rationing out grain for the horses and then looking over the surrounding area on foot. He returned to the fire frequently to warm up and brought with him each time an armload of greasewood, building up fuel for the long, cold night.

As they were eating in the growing darkness, light flakes of snow began sifting down.

"I had a feeling," intoned the lawman mournfully.

"Hap said he could always feel in his bones

when it was going to snow," Christie said, refilling the marshal's coffee cup from the fire-blackened pot.

She returned to her seat by the fire. A light dusting of snowflakes settled on the shoulders of her coat and she shivered. "I just can't seem to get all the way warmed up," she said, hugging herself with her thin arms.

Cooper stood up, peeled off his coat, and draped it around her.

"I can't take yer coat!" she protested.

"Wear it for a while," he ordered. "I'm going to throw us together some kind of shelter so we don't have to sleep in the snow." Had she been up to her usual healthy state, her own coat would have been more than sufficient. Though her brow puckered in disapproval, Christie drew the warm fleece-lined coat about her, drawing her face into its cozy warmth. She sighed contentedly.

While Christie hugged the fire, Cooper draped his canvas tarp between two large, upright boulders, and secured its edges with small rocks around the perimeter. It would suffice to keep their beds free of the falling snow, provided the snow did not accumulate so heavily as to pull the tarp loose and dump its load upon the two of them.

Cooper spread out their bedrolls beneath the tarp and together they sat beneath its shelter, basking in the warmth of the fire and the restful comfort of the moment.

Cooper was tired. He felt the weary miles and the cold and the nagging effects of all they had been through settle into him. Oddly, he also felt at peace. Maybe it was just the warmth of the crackling fire, the contented blowing of the horses. Maybe it was the close presence of the girl. His own temperament was plodding, methodical — the girl brought a sweet sparkle to his usually grim world. Throughout her ordeal she had retained a snap of defiance that could not be beaten down. In their days together, Cooper had yet to hear a complaint pass her lips. More often, it was a joke, a lighthearted comment, or pointing out to the lawman some newly discovered marvel in her young life.

Old Hap had done one hell of a job raising the girl. But it was Christie herself who was the vessel — and a vessel without a single leak, at that. She knew who she was, and though she might not know where it was she was going in life, she would get there, and in fine style too.

"I know where the money is, Marshal." Her voice was soft, so drowsy that for a moment it seemed as though she had but mumbled in her sleep. But then the awareness of what she had said struck him.

"What did you say?" he asked stupidly, setting his cup on the ground beside his bedroll.

"One time when he was talking about sending me to school in Denver he told me. Hap told me never to tell no one else, no matter what. But since this trip might be both our undoing, I think it might be a good idea for you to know. That way, if one of us gets out, then he can at least have the money."

"You mean all this time you knew and you didn't let on?" Cooper was astounded. "You let that old man die and you didn't say a word?"

"Hap told me never to tell," she said simply. "No matter what. Besides, they would've killed him anyways. An' once they had the money they'd've killed me too, after they used me up. I did just what I had to do, Marshal."

Cooper stared blankly at her. "I'll be damned," he murmured. "I'll just plain be damned."

"You ain't mad at me, Marshal, are you? Hap was the one what told me to keep quiet. Even while they was torturing him, he kept lookin' at me with those mean eyes of his, warnin' me to keep shut."

Cooper answered finally, "How could I be mad? I'm just surprised as hell, though." He saw the hurt look in her eyes. "It isn't your fault, Christie. You were right. If you had told, you'd be dead now, too. You did the right thing."

She nodded gratefully. "I'm glad you ain't mad. I'm real fond of you, Marshal. After all you went through to get me away from them animals — nearly gettin' yourself killed an' all."

Cooper looked at her and saw her simple, weathered face, oval in shape, eyes blue and wide-set, small nose with a sprinkle of freckles, a resolute jaw with a cupid's bow mouth. She had changed, in their short time together, from a girl-child to a young woman. Tough times will do that to people, rapid acceleration of growth in spirit, toughening of fiber. And, by God, Christie had had her share of those tough times. Yet, as he looked into those clear, bright eyes, he saw a softness that would never be driven out by suffering and ill-treatment — tenderness unassailable.

Cooper smiled at the girl. "I'm fond of you too, Christie. You're quite a gal. And a pretty one, too," he added with a wink.

A tinge of red mounted Christie's cheeks, and she turned from his gaze to look into the flames.

The snow continued to fall, small, silent flakes muting and whitening the ragged landscape. It was nearly warm in the makeshift shelter, the heat being reflected within by the

277

large boulders behind the fire.

"Are you married, Marshal?" Christie asked, eyes still buried in the flames.

He looked at her, but she avoided his eyes. A warning bell went off in his brain.

"Been close to it," he answered. "One of those things a careful man keeps putting off until everything is just right."

"You got a woman waitin'?"

Cooper nodded. "And waitin' and waitin'. Any day now I expect her to tell me to get on down the road. Neither of us is getting any younger."

Christie opened her mouth to speak but Cooper cut her off, answering her anticipated question. "I'm thirty-six in February," he said. "Not exactly senile yet, but I haven't got all that many good years left, either."

"Shoot, that ain't old," she commented cheerily. "You're just gettin' seasoned good."

Cooper smiled at that, got up and refilled his coffee cup, then threw more wood on the fire. The fine snow continued to sift down.

"I got somethin' to say to you, Marshal . . . Ben," she began with a nervous glance in his direction. "Somethin' I been thinkin' about for a few days now."

Again the warning bell sounded. "Maybe you ought to sleep on it a bit longer," he advised, starting his coffee cup to his lips, then returning it untasted to his lap.

"No. It needs to be said," she insisted. "It's either there or it ain't. Stewin' over it ain't going to help — just drag it out. All I ask is you let me say it all, without interruptin'. Is that a deal?"

"Speak on, gal. All we're missing is a good night's sleep."

She took a deep breath. "Ben —" she said the name softly, almost reverently, "tomorrow is my birthday. I'll be sixteen. I figure that's about nineteen years difference in our ages. And that ain't nothin' at all. Lot of married couples are farther apart than that."

He stifled a groan, resolving to hear her out. She was speaking openly, honestly, and without embarrassment. He warned himself he must not injure her dignity. She was in a grown-up world now, and she warranted the respect and attention of an adult woman.

"You said you got you another woman. Well, that's just fine. But it seems to me if things were all that hot between you, you would have been married by now."

The thought gave Cooper a sudden jolt. She had said outright something he had been unwilling to admit to himself for years.

"I just want you to know I'm throwin' my hat in the ring." She had picked up an uneaten biscuit from the tin plate beside her and was shredding it unmercifully. "There. That's said." She took a deep breath. "There's one more thing you need to be thinkin' about. There's all that money back there. After all these years, there's no way of knowin' or findin' out who it belonged to. I didn't have nothin' to do with stealin' it, but I figure I got just as much claim to it as the next person.

"We could take that money, Ben, and start us out somewhere with a ranch or a business. There's plenty of money for either one, or both."

She hesitated, frowning. "It ain't easy talkin' about feelin's. But I guess I should tell you I admire and respect you and . . . love you." She looked up from the destruction of the biscuit, eyes pensive, uncertain, lips trembling with the emotion boiling within her.

Cooper was surprised to notice he felt no embarrassment himself. Her total honesty had somehow knocked away that scaffold of artificiality people construct to protect their feelings.

"Like I said, Christie, you're quite a gal." He paused, searching. He had to be careful. "Let's take the things you mentioned. The age thing, the difference in our years. Now *that* would bother me, what people were saying about us."

"We could move away —"

He raised a hand, cutting her off. "I heard you out," he said gently. "Now it's my turn."

He paused another moment, framing his thoughts. When he spoke again his tone was firm, businesslike.

"The woman waiting back in Mexican Hat — you might just be right about that situation. I knew there was something holding us back, some good reason for waiting. I just wasn't sure what it was. I think you just might've hit on it. But I've got to work things out myself with Jane. I owe her that. I owe it to myself. You've made me see that, and I thank you for it."

She threw the biscuit scraps into the fire, drew her legs up, and clasped her hands below her knees.

"Are you turning me down?" she asked bluntly.

"Christie," he said gently. "There's too many years difference. You're too young, girl. You'll change your mind a dozen times before you finally settle on the right man."

"You're sayin' I'm a child what don't know her own mind," she said, tears running down her cheeks.

"I'm saying you're a young woman just starting to blossom out. I know a lot of girls marry at your age. And a good many of them spend the rest of their lives regretting it.

You're talking about a big step. Give yourself some time, Christie."

She stared into the fire, sullen and morose.

"When this is all over," he said, "think about it some more. You'll see I'm right."

Christie pulled off her boots and rolled in her blankets, her face turned away from the lawman.

Cooper shrugged and settled into his own bed, arranging his six-gun close to hand.

"One thing you might as well know," she muttered, her voice muffled by the blankets. "You might as well know where the money's hid. Neither one of us has got any guarantee about making it back to Mexican Hat alive, but if one of us makes it, at least he'll git the use of the money."

Her face still turned away from him, she said, "There's an old well, 'bout a hundred yards off from the new one Hap dug. It's all dried out and there's a ladder runnin' down into it. 'Bout half-way down — sides are all rocked up — there's a big rock in the wall. The money's stashed in a hole behind the rock."

"Should it happen I find it," Cooper said after a moment's silence, "I'll have to turn it in. You know that."

Silence settled over the camp. The snow turned to sleet and the little slivers of ice pecked at the canvas tarpaulin over their beds. The fire sputtered. Inside the shelter it was warm and peaceful.

Cooper felt himself relax. His back, the area of the wound, ached a bit, but the warmth of his bed felt good, and he felt the tensions draining away.

"That being the case," said Christie in a sleepy voice, "pray God I get to it first." A moment later she was snoring softly, the tears on her cheeks already dry.

THORNDIKE PRESS hopes you have enjoyed this Large Print book. All our Large Print titles are designed for easy reading, and all our books are made to last. Other Thorndike Large Print books are available at your library, through selected bookstores, or directly from the publisher. For more information about current and upcoming titles, please call or mail your name and address to:

THORNDIKE PRESS
PO Box 159
Thorndike, Maine 04986
800/223-6121
207/948-2962